Danger in the Dogwoods

Jenna Maeson

Dedicated to:

The original Elmer inspiration, Paddington. You will always be the goodest boy.

March 2010 – December 2024

contents

PROLOGUE

The buzz around Emerald Ridge was palpable. For weeks, a single event consumed the sleepy town. This event, the wedding of Jill Hastings and Desmond Montgomery, promised to bring both excitement and chaos to the quiet mountain community. Jill, a high-society darling with a flair for the extravagant, was marrying Desmond, a powerful attorney whose name circulated among the elite. Dogwood Cottage, an idyllic estate just outside of town, was to host their wedding.

But it wasn't just the high-profile couple that had everyone talking—it was the fact that Jill, of all people, had kept it "local." She'd insisted on hiring residents from Emerald Ridge for everything. It was as if a lightning bolt hit the town square; everyone from the diner's cook to the botanist was pulled into the whirlwind of wedding prep, whether or not they were ready.

They somehow roped Raymond Filtch, the gruff yet dependable owner of the town's beloved diner, into catering. He'd never forget the day he was informed that his usual menu of pancakes and meatloaf wouldn't cut it for this crowd. "I don't even know what a 'foie gras crostini' is!" he had muttered, baffled, as he wiped his hands on his apron.

Meanwhile, they tasked Edward Barnes, the town's eccentric botanist, with curating "exotic florals" for the big day. The word "exotic" had sent him into a three-day research spiral, scouring every corner of the internet for flowers that screamed wealth, class, and just a pinch of over-the-top opulence.

Then there was Ashley, the cheery, ever-present face at Perks and Peaks, Emerald Ridge's coffee shop. She and her family had been commissioned to set up a custom coffee bar for the wedding weekend. She joked that if she heard the word "handcrafted espresso blend" one more time, she might lose it.

Olivia Morgan, newly returned to Emerald Ridge, found herself swept up in the excitement as well, assigned a role perfectly suited to her abilities. Hired to pet-sit for Jill's prized poodle, Chardonnay, Olivia knew she had a challenge on her hands. Chardonnay, a pampered show dog with a diva streak, was demanding enough to make anyone question their career choices. Olivia had expected the usual job of caring for one or two pets—but no, Jill had offered Olivia's services to the bridal party as well, which meant wrangling a menagerie of spoiled animals throughout the weekend. Even though Olivia had doubts, she was in it for the paycheck, which would cover her bills for months to come. And who could turn down a job like that, no matter how chaotic?

Despite the grumbling and eye-rolling from the townsfolk, no one could deny it: this wedding was the biggest thing to hit Emerald Ridge in a long time. And while the rest of the world would focus on the romance of the event, the residents of Emerald Ridge knew better—there was bound to be more going on behind the scenes than a simple exchange of vows.

But no one was prepared for what was about to unfold.

CHAPTER 1

Olivia adjusted her rearview mirror, giving herself a fleeting glance before focusing on the road ahead. "This is it," she muttered under her breath as the Jeep bounced along the gravel path. Flanked by towering dogwood trees, their branches heavy with delicate blossoms, the driveway wound its way toward the sprawling estate—Dogwood Cottage. But calling it a "cottage" was like calling a mansion a "fixer-upper."

Elmer, her large golden retriever mix and trusty sidekick, pressed his nose against the window, taking in the unfamiliar sights, clearly intrigued by what was unfolding before them.

She eased past the circular drive, slowing to absorb the full grandeur of the place. The stone façade gleamed under the soft afternoon light, ivy climbing its way up the walls. Massive arched windows reflected the vibrant pinks and whites of the surrounding dogwood blossoms. In the center of the drive, a fountain bubbled over with an excessive number of lilies.

Olivia parked in the gravel lot, marked Guest Parking and killed the engine, giving Elmer a quick once-over. "Ready to meet our new client?" she asked. Ever the adventurer, Elmer thumped his tail enthusiastically.

Stepping out, Olivia inhaled deeply as Elmer clambered out behind her. The air was thick with the sweet scent of dogwood blossoms, their fragrance mingling with the crisp breeze rustling through the trees. It was an intoxicating aroma that only enhanced the estate's serene beauty.

As she made her way toward the entrance, her shoes crunching on the gravel, Olivia couldn't help but feel out of place. Her usual pet-sitting gigs involved muddy paw prints on hardwood floors and slobbery kisses from lovable mutts—not this kind of high-brow affair with pets that probably had better grooming schedules than she did.

She squinted at the extravagant floral arrangements towering over the entryway, wondering if she was stepping into a wedding venue or a nature documentary. Glancing down at Elmer, who eyed the manicured hedges with interest, she muttered, "Don't even think about it," giving his leash a gentle tug.

The double doors swung open, and a whirlwind of energy hit her like a blast of cold air.

Jill Hastings stood framed in the doorway, exuding the kind of intensity that screamed bride on a mission. Immaculate and poised, she balanced her phone in one hand and a color-coded wedding planner in the other. Her designer dress, tailored to perfection and likely worth more than Olivia's Jeep, shimmered in the sunlight.

"You must be Olivia," Jill said, her smile tight. "I'm so glad you're here. We've been… well, waiting. There's a lot to go over today."

Olivia returned the smile politely. "Nice to meet you, Jill."

Jill's gaze flicked over Olivia's worn jeans and well-loved Converse, lingering briefly before moving to Elmer, who sat obediently at her side. She arched an eyebrow. "And this is Elmer, I assume?" she asked, her tone polite but detached—like she was evaluating whether he met her high standards for a dog.

Olivia patted Elmer's head. "Yes, this is Elmer."

As if on cue, Elmer raised a paw in an enthusiastic attempt at a handshake. Jill's eyebrows shot up. She stepped back, a small frown tugging at the corners of her mouth.

Elmer, clearly unimpressed by the rejection, let out an exaggerated sigh before flopping on the floor with a dramatic huff.

"Charming," Jill remarked flatly. "Elmer is… unique. Where did the name come from?"

Olivia's chest tightened. "He was my best friend Emily's dog before she passed away a few months ago." Saying Emily's name still felt like a weight pressing against her lungs, but she kept her voice steady.

She glanced down at Elmer, a memory surfacing—Emily's laughter, bright and full of life. "When she first got him, she used to tell me how he followed her everywhere, stuck to her like glue. She'd stop, and he'd crash into her every time." Olivia smiled softly, recalling the videos Emily had sent—Elmer's unwavering loyalty, his big brown eyes always watching her every move. "She didn't name him right away, but eventually, she settled on 'Elmer,' like Elmer's Glue, because he never left her side."

Jill's pause stretched a beat too long, thick with unspoken thoughts. Finally, she forced a smile. "How quaint."

She shifted her stance, clearly eager to move the conversation along. "Now, Chardonnay—my poodle—is your primary charge. She's in my suite at the moment." Jill turned on her heel and motioned for Olivia to follow. "I'll take you to her. She's my absolute darling and requires all your attention. I'm sure I don't have to tell you how important she is to me."

Olivia nodded, keeping pace

"Now that you're here, we can move her to your cottage. The other pets will stay there as well. It has two bedrooms, but one is reserved specifically for Chardonnay. The others will just have to make do."

As they stepped into the grand foyer, Olivia took in her surroundings. The ceilings stretched impossibly high, and the marble floors gleamed so flawlessly she could see her own reflection. Crystal chandeliers hung above them like glittering behemoths, making everything feel larger than life.

"Here we are," Jill said, leading Olivia down a hallway and stopping in front of a polished oak door. "I'm counting on you, Olivia. Without her, the entire wedding will fall apart."

No pressure, Olivia thought.

Jill pushed open the door with a flourish, revealing a suite that could have easily been mistaken for a five-star hotel room. The space was pristine, bathed in soft, golden light streaming through the expansive windows. But it was the corner of the room that captured Olivia's attention.

Nestled amidst plush cushions and rich tapestries, was an entire setup dedicated solely to Chardonnay. A plush, oversized dog bed—nearly as large as the extravagant four-poster bed centered in the room—sat by the window, offering an ideal view of the sprawling estate. Embroidered with intricate gold threads, it looked almost regal. Beside it, a marble water fountain bubbled softly, its crystal-clear water shimmering in the sunlight.

The room smelled faintly of lavender and something earthy, but it was the sight of the dog that stopped Olivia in her tracks.

Chardonnay, a sleek and impeccably groomed standard poodle, lay sprawled across the dog bed. Her snow-white coat gleamed with the gloss of top-tier grooming, her perfectly trimmed curls catching the soft light. She lifted her head just enough to acknowledge Olivia and Elmer, making it clear she was well aware of her surroundings. Her large, dark eyes regarded them with mild interest and a perceptible air of superiority.

Elmer, standing beside Olivia, sniffed the air and gave the poodle a curious glance. He huffed softly, as if questioning whether the animal before him was truly a canine. His usual laid-back demeanor remained unshaken by the extravagant surroundings.

Olivia murmured, "There she is—Chardonnay, the star of the show." Her voice was low, more to herself than anyone else, but Jill overheard and beamed, completely missing the hint of sarcasm.

"I know, right? Isn't she just perfect?" Jill said, settling onto a low bench at the foot of the bed. She called to Chardonnay, who hesitated for a moment before rising from her plush throne and trotting over, placing her paws delicately on Jill's lap to receive the attention she was clearly accustomed to.

"She's the star of the ceremony, of course. The wedding wouldn't move forward without her." Jill ran her fingers through Chardonnay's white fur, smiling at her fondly. Then, with a note of urgency, she looked at Olivia. "You'll keep her comfortable, won't you? She gets stressed with too much chaos."

Olivia resisted the urge to ask what counted as chaos in Jill's world and how much of it Chardonnay had ever actually experienced.

She could feel her own smile falter as she watched Jill fawn over the dog. Chardonnay, unbothered, blinked up at Olivia—who had the distinct feeling, without a single word exchanged, that the poodle expected her to adopt the same level of devotion.

As Jill continued speaking to her dog in a sing-song voice, Olivia took in the rest of the room. The suite was a testament to opulence, exuding refined elegance. Rich velvet drapes framed the floor-to-ceiling windows, which offered a sweeping view of the estate's manicured grounds. The walls, painted in soft shades of cream and gold, reflected the warm, inviting light that poured in from the windows.

At the center of the room, a king-sized four-poster bed dominated the space, draped in silky linens and an extravagant array of plush pillows. The headboard, upholstered in deep burgundy velvet, added a touch of dramatic luxury.

An ornate crystal chandelier hung from the ceiling, its sparkling facets casting a soft glow across the space. The polished wood floors gleamed, and a soft rug lay at the foot of the bed, adding a touch of warmth. Beside the bed, a mahogany vanity with an intricate mirror stood adorned with neatly arranged perfume bottles, gold-trimmed picture frames, and the occasional stray flower from one of the lavish floral arrangements Jill favored.

Across from the bed, a chaise lounge, clad in the same burgundy velvet as the headboard, invited relaxation. It was positioned beside a curated collection of art pieces that adorned the walls—abstract, yet tasteful. The suite was an oasis of indulgence, a space that left no detail overlooked, from the plush bedding to the carefully selected décor.

Olivia and Elmer were undeniably out of their element, more accustomed to the warmth of well-worn comfort than the gleam and polish of extravagance. She could hear Elmer's thoughts: *Do people actually live like this? Why? Doesn't seem comfortable.* With an exaggerated sigh, he plopped onto the floor at Olivia's feet, making it clear that, in his opinion, this little meet-and-greet had long exceeded its time limit.

"Not quite what you're used to, huh, buddy?" Olivia whispered, reaching down to give Elmer a reassuring pat. He glanced up at her, his wide eyes betraying his bewilderment at the grandeur surrounding them.

Jill, catching Olivia's amused glance, straightened with a satisfied expression. "Because Chardonnay loves the space I set up for her in my suite, I replicated it exactly in her room at your cottage," she said proudly. "She's my world, and I want everything to be perfect for her. And for the wedding, of course," she added, almost as an afterthought.

Olivia could only nod, her thoughts already drifting toward the reality of her situation: high-society obsession, a wedding so extravagant it bordered on absurd, and a dog that would likely steal the spotlight from the bride herself. Judging by the way Jill spoke, it seemed that was the plan all along.

Jill turned her attention to Elmer, still sprawled on the floor in complete indifference. "And I trust you'll make sure Elmer doesn't get any ideas," she added, raising an eyebrow. "Chardonnay is a beautiful girl with champion bloodlines."

Elmer, oblivious to any of the implications, remained unbothered. His eyes briefly flicked toward Chardonnay—curious, yet unimpressed—before he closed them again, clearly uninterested in the drama unfolding around him.

"I'll be around if you need anything, of course," Jill said with an air of finality. "My assistant will bring Chardonnay down to your cottage a little later." She gestured toward the door. "Let me know if there's anything else. Just... keep her calm, okay?"

Olivia gave a tight but polite smile. "Got it." She glanced down at Elmer, whose thoughts mirrored her own: *This is going to be a long weekend.*

Just as Olivia was about to step out, Jill seemed to reconsider dismissing them. "Before you settle in, let me introduce you to my fiancé, Desmond, and the rest of the bridal party. They should all be out on the lawn practicing their spacing and pacing for the ceremony. Follow me."

CHAPTER 2

Olivia and Elmer followed Jill out onto the manicured lawn of Dogwood Cottage. Olivia adjusted Elmer's leash and tried to suppress a sigh. This wasn't any old wedding, this was the kind of wedding where even the flowers were too fancy for their own good. Jill walked determinedly down the cobblestone path to the patio where the bridal party had assembled. Olivia wondered how anyone could walk so quickly in such high heels.

"Olivia!" Jill waved her over with a manicured hand. "Come, I want you to meet everyone."

Olivia forced a polite smile, glancing down at Elmer, who seemed to sense her discomfort and let out a slight huff, nudging her leg.

Jill gestured to the small group gathered around her, clutching the arm of a striking male figure. "This is my fiancé, Desmond Montgomery."

Desmond stood next to her, wearing a tailored suit that screamed 'high-powered attorney.' He extended a hand toward Olivia with a charming but distant smile, his eyes scanning her before shifting back to Jill. "Olivia, thanks for helping with the pets. I know Jill's been worried about Chardonnay." His voice was smooth, the kind of voice that probably won cases before the arguments even started. "It's been helpful for everyone involved, knowing they could bring their pets along and leave them in expert hands." Olivia arched an eyebrow at that. Jill suggested a couple of extra pets beyond Chardonnay, but she seemed to have downplayed things a bit.

"Nice to meet you," Olivia said, shaking his hand. "I'm sure everything will go smoothly."

"And this is Monica," Jill continued, gesturing to the woman standing on the other side of Desmond.

Monica Montgomery—maid of honor and Desmond's younger sister—looked like she'd rather be anywhere else. Dressed in an immaculate sheath dress, she had a sharpness about her, with eyes that seemed to note every person's every move. There was something tense about her posture, like she was holding her breath. The resemblance between her and her brother was striking, from the dark hair to the angular faces, as was the height difference. Monica looked to be slightly over five feet tall and Desmond was well over six feet.

"Olivia, right? The pet sitter?" Monica's smile was thin and polite, but something about her tone felt off.

"That's me," Olivia said, matching her tone with a lightness of her own. Monica glanced down at Elmer and reached out a hand to pet him. The normally gregarious Elmer shrunk back, away from her hand, looking at her warily. *That's odd*, thought Olivia. She had never seen Elmer act that way towards anyone. He normally treated everyone like a friend he hadn't met yet. Monica looked offended by the rebuff but retracted her hand and stepped back.

"Sorry about that, "said Olivia. "He's not always comfortable in new places."

Monica nodded curtly, then her gaze flicked to Desmond for just a second before she turned back to Jill. "With Olivia here, the pets may be the one thing we don't have to worry about during this wedding. Right, Des?"

Desmond's jaw tightened, but his smile remained intact. "We've got everything under control, Monica, but I'm sure that Olivia will be a great help."

Jill, blissfully unaware of the tension between her fiancé and his sister, continued introducing the rest of the wedding party—Shara, Katherine, and Rachel, the bridesmaids, and Seth, Marco, and Victor, the groomsmen. A pet also accompanied most members of the bridal party, some looking more thrilled to have them along than others. As Jill finished the introductions, she clapped her hands together. "Great! Now that we're all acquainted, Olivia, I trust you'll make sure Chardonnay is ready for her big moment in the wedding procession."

At the mention of the star of the show, the parrot perched on Katherine's shoulder broke out in a rendition of "Somewhere Over the Rainbow". Katherine chuckled, saying, "Oh Tulip, you silly girl. I know you are used to being the star, but it's ok if you aren't in the spotlight all the time. Jill already has a star. You have your...small...part to do, and I'm sure you will be perfect." Katherine may have meant her comment to be light-hearted, but Olivia felt a tinge of annoyance running underneath her words. Jill did not seem amused. "Katherine, make sure she sticks to the script for her part. I don't need any of this ad-libbing to steal Chardonnay's spotlight." Jill turned back to Olivia, but Olivia caught Katherine rolling her eyes as soon as Jill had turned her back.

Olivia forced a smile, suppressing a chuckle. "I'll make sure everyone is taken care of," she said, but her thoughts were already elsewhere. Glancing around, anxiety built in her stomach. She was used to handling animals, but this was a lot. A parrot, a dachshund, a Pitbull, and a cat along with Chardonnay, all who presumably had their own "part" in the wedding. She was starting to wonder what she had gotten herself into. Jill had an almost absurd attachment to Chardonnay, treating her as though the dog was the real guest of honor—part of the elaborate spectacle

Jill seemed to believe was essential to the wedding. "The others will bring their pets down to you after we all practice our parts in the ceremony!" She sounded more delighted by the prospect than any of the wedding party or their pets looked.

Jill glanced around, her gaze sweeping over the group of bridesmaids and groomsmen. The best man, Marco, was inspecting his tie, and Victor and Seth, the other groomsmen, looked unengaged with the ongoing instructions. "And I'm sure you'll make the other pets as comfortable as possible," Jill added, her eyes lingering on Olivia with a mix of expectation and pride, as though the entire wedding hinged on the comfort of the pets.

It was clear—Jill's obsession with animals went far beyond the norm. These were not mere pets; they were participants in the ceremony, incorporated into the fabric of the day. Even the thought of not having Chardonnay play her role in the wedding was unthinkable for Jill.

Olivia's head spun as she took in the full scope of the wedding party's animal involvement. But she also couldn't ignore the undercurrent of tension in the air—Monica's biting words, Desmond's strained smile, and Jill's almost frantic energy were already giving her a glimpse of the cracks just beneath the polished surface of this extravagant affair. It was one thing to treat pets like family, but there was something deeper at play. Olivia had been around long enough to know when things were about to go sideways.

As the introductions wrapped up, Jill gave Olivia a reassuring smile. "Thank you for helping, Olivia. Now, if you need anything, don't hesitate to ask! You know, it's so rare to find someone who understands the importance of pet involvement in life's special moments."

Olivia smiled politely, but her gaze briefly caught Monica's, who was staring at her brother with an unreadable expression. Olivia wasn't sure what it was, but she had a feeling this wedding was about to become a lot more complicated.

Jill dismissed Olivia and Elmer to go "settle in" but before they had made their way to the path leading to the cottage, Olivia heard Jill's phone ping with a message. Olivia watched as she checked her phone. Turning to Desmond, she said, "Honey, the Incandescent ivory tablecloths are out of stock at the last minute. I need to pick another color and pay the rush fee to get them here in time. It's going to be an extra thousand dollars, it looks like." Jill looked expectantly at Desmond, who shifted from side to side as he reached for his wallet. He pulled out his wallet and handed Jill a gold credit card. "Of course dear, whatever you need.", he replied casually, though his expression was anything but. Jill gave him a quick kiss on the cheek and then directed the wedding party to their indicated areas on the lawn before stepping away to make her call to the linen supplier. Olivia glanced around, noticing that Monica seemed to have disappeared, and as soon as Jill turned away, she saw Desmond slinking off as well. *That's strange*, Olivia thought, as she and Elmer made their way to the path heading towards the cottage.

As Elmer and Olivia rounded the corner of the back porch of Dogwood Cottage, Olivia heard a tense conversation and slowed her approach. She saw Desmond, drink in hand, leaning against the veranda, gazing out at the estate. Monica approached from behind him, her heels clicking on the wooden floorboards. He didn't need to turn around to know it was her. Olivia slowed, pressing herself and Elmer to the side of the building just behind the porch railing. Elmer looked at her quizzically and Olivia pressed her finger to her lips to make sure he stayed silent.

"You seem tense, Des," Monica said, her voice a low, cool whisper. She sidled up beside him, her lips curved into a smile that didn't match the sharpness in her eyes. "Big wedding jitters? Or is it something else?"

Desmond clenched his jaw, glancing over at his sister. "Is this what you are going to do all weekend, Monica? Follow me around, throwing veiled threats in whenever you have the chance? "

Monica's smile widened, but there was no humor in it. She leaned in closer, her voice dropping to an even softer whisper. "I suppose they aren't very well veiled if you realize they are threats. I just want to make sure our agreement remains at the forefront of your mind. You have as much riding on this as I do."

Desmond stiffened. "I know.," said Desmond, exasperated. "I've talked to him, but he just isn't taking the bait easily." Olivia saw Desmond run his hands through his hair. "And if Jill keeps having wedding "emergencies" I need to pay for, I don't know...", his voice trailed off. "I feel like I'm mortgaging our future for this wedding."

Monica let out a soft, breathy laugh, resting her hand on the railing beside him. "You mean that shiny gold card hasn't been the key to solving all of your problems?"

Desmond huffed a humorless laugh, "Hardly."

Monica's smile faltered and her eyes darkened. "You're so good at business, aren't you, Desmond? Your entire career built on that dazzling legal mind of yours. I'm sure you will figure a way to get this done."

Desmond's face flushed. "Monica — don't forget what you've got riding on this as well. The image and lifestyle you've curated so carefully could come crashing down at any moment. We are in this together."

"Of course," she responded. "As long as we close this deal, there will be no issues, and you will ride off into the sunset with your beautiful bride." She straightened, brushing an imaginary speck of dust off her dress. "Because if I go down, Desmond, you're coming with me. We both understand its impact on your career and future with Jill. Knowing the truth, why would she choose you?"

Monica paused before stepping away, turning back to Desmond with a sharp look. "This isn't just about you and me, Des. It's about the Montgomery family name. Mom and Dad would turn in their graves if they knew everything they left us was at risk. We haven't exactly handled the estate the way they would have wanted. We can't afford to tarnish their legacy." She let the weight of her remarks linger for a moment before adding, "Jill mentioned a reporter who's attending the wedding—Thomas, I think his name is. Apparently, he reached out a while back, wanting to write a piece about the merging of the Hastings and Montgomery names. I'm not sure if he's just here for some fluff article or something more serious." Monica's lips curved into a small smile. "I did a little digging. He seems to lean more toward investigative journalism than light gossip. Maybe he'd be interested in our family's… secrets." She shot him a final, mocking smile. "Make sure I don't have to talk to him." Desmond watched her walk away, her words hanging in the air like a noose tightening around his neck.

Once Olivia was sure the coast was clear, she and Elmer continued down the path toward the guest accommodations. The weight of Monica's comments still lingered in Olivia's mind. She had sensed something off between Monica and Desmond when they met, but the conversation she overheard sounded much bigger than a simple sibling spat. Monica had implied that Desmond, one of the most powerful lawyers in the area, wasn't what he seemed. Olivia shook her head, trying to shake off the nagging thought.

Don't get involved, she told herself. *You're here for the pets, not the drama.*

A twist of unease tightened her chest, but she was determined to focus on the task at hand.

CHAPTER 3

Towering dogwood trees sheltered the guest cottages scattered across the estate's rolling hills. Each cottage was a picture of understated elegance, constructed from warm stone and dark wood, blending harmoniously with the lush landscape. Ivy climbed their walls, giving them the illusion of being part of the earth, while wide porches, adorned with wicker furniture and hanging flower baskets, invited guests to relax and soak in the tranquil mountain views.

Inside, the cottages exuded comfort without being pretentious. Wooden beams arched across the ceilings, and large stone fireplaces took center stage in the living rooms, offering a cozy refuge on cool evenings. Polished hardwood floors stretched through the rooms, softened by luxurious rugs and comfortable seating. The décor balanced rustic charm with modern convenience—plush bedding, state-of-the-art kitchenettes that Olivia doubted many guests use, and sleek, minimalist furnishings that felt both luxurious and warm.

Each cottage boasted its own unique view of the estate. Some overlooked the sprawling gardens, others enjoyed a view of a small, serene lake shimmering in the distance. A winding path connected all the cottages to the main house, ensuring guests could enjoy both privacy and proximity to the heart of their event.

Olivia's cottage, nestled at the far edge of the estate, offered more seclusion than the others. It was likely reserved for her because of the pet-sitting duties, but the quiet was a welcome touch. The charming cottage offered two bedrooms, weathered shutters, and a porch swing. Tall trees surrounded it, their pine scent mingling with the sweet fragrance of the blossoming dogwoods.

The cottage's interior was thoughtfully divided into two parts. The first bedroom, which had a sign reading "Chardonnay's Quarters" hanging on the door, was a shrine to the bride's pampered pooch. Olivia couldn't help but raise an eyebrow at the over-the-top setup. As Jill had mentioned, the space set up for Chardonnay was an exact replica of what was in Jill's suite—right down to the bubbling marble fountain.

Only for Chardonnay, Olivia thought dryly, glancing at Elmer, who snorted and padded off toward the second bedroom. A practical room, it featured a comfortable bed near a large window framing the estate; no silk or chandeliers. Elmer claimed his spot on the bed, settling in to watch the landscape intently.

The main room opened into a spacious living area with wide windows that let in floods of light. A large stone fireplace served as the room's centerpiece, surrounded by comfortable couches and chairs. Plush pet beds, already set up for the other animals, were scattered across the room; a small shelf holding pet supplies—treats, grooming kits, and leashes—sat beside the door. The earthy tones of the room, combined with the soft lighting and warm atmosphere, made it feel like a cozy haven.

As Olivia set her things down in the second bedroom, she gave Elmer a sideways glance. "Looks like we'll have a few more... guests."

Elmer dramatically sighed, resigned to the fact that his peace and quiet would soon be disrupted.

Olivia surveyed the room with mixed amusement and dread. "This place is nicer than any place I've ever stayed, let alone lived," she muttered, shaking her head.

Elmer's thoughts were clear as day: *Better enjoy it while it lasts.*

"I guess so," Olivia chuckled, scratching his ears. Olivia reached down to unpack their bags, and she heard her phone ping from inside her back pocket. She pulled it out, glancing at the screen, and couldn't contain a smile.

Noah: *Did you make it out to that wedding place?*

Olivia perched on the edge of the bed to type her reply.

Olivia: *Yeah, Elmer and I made it. We are settling into our cottage.* As an afterthought, she added, *When are you headed up here?*

Jill had enlisted Noah to fix up a classic car as the "getaway car" for the wedding. From what she had heard from Noah, the car had needed more than a little fixing up. He would drive the car up to the wedding site prior to the wedding festivities. Olivia hoped she didn't sound overeager, but for whatever reason, since she had been back in town, she had been enjoying Noah's company, more than a little.

Noah: *I'm supposed to bring the car up the evening of the rehearsal dinner. Jill gave me a cottage to stay in for the night.*

Olivia smiled. The thought of having Noah close by put her at ease. Then she heard Elmer's thoughts cut through her dreamy haze. *Noah?* Olivia turned to look at him. "How did you know?," she asked. *You act funny when it's Noah,* came his response. Olivia shook her head. *Was it really that obvious?*

She had just finished unpacking Elmer's things—his bowls, toys, and an assortment of treats—when the sound of expensive heels clicking against the porch reached her ears. She glanced up to see Jill standing in the doorway, a vision of poise and elegance, her platinum hair styled in soft waves, her outfit remaining spotless and perfectly pressed, no matter how much she had been running around. Over-sized sunglasses perched on her head as she stepped inside, Chardonnay at her side, looking every bit as regal as her owner. A bedazzled collar and matching leash, more like fine jewelry than dog accessories, adorned the standard poodle.

"Olivia, darling," Jill cooed, stepping into the cottage, her perfume filling the air. "I thought I'd bring her down myself. Just wanted to make sure everything was perfect for her." Chardonnay padded inside, taking a few measured steps into the room as if inspecting her surroundings.

Elmer poked his head out of the second room to see who their visitors were. His gaze landed on the fluffy white dog. Realizing these were visitors he had already met, he disappeared back into the room to return to his nap without further comment.

Chardonnay sniffed one of Elmer's toys before lifting her nose and scanning her surroundings, immediately identifying which bedroom was hers and making herself at home.

Jill followed the dog's every movement, eyes gleaming with adoration. "I made sure everything was perfect for her. She deserves the best." She turned toward Olivia. "When I asked around for pet-sitting recommendations, your name kept coming up, and I knew Chardonnay would be in good hands with you."

Olivia forced a smile, trying to keep the absurdity of the situation in check. *Being the only pet-sitter around the area, that makes sense,* Olivia thought to herself, but Jill didn't need to know that. Still, she kept her tone light. "Of course, Jill. I'll treat her like royalty.

Jill chuckled, though there was an edge to it. "Oh, you better! I've spent more time arranging her accommodations than my own." She adjusted her sunglasses, giving Olivia a pointed look. "Chardonnay is the centerpiece of the wedding, after all. Can you imagine anything more adorable than her walking down the aisle with flowers in her fur?"

Olivia kept her smile intact, though her mind was racing. "Nothing could be cuter. I'm sure it will be perfect."

Jill, satisfied, clapped her hands as Chardonnay trotted over to her extravagant bed and circled before lying down with a contented sigh. Jill looked at her dog, lost in the moment of perfection. "Perfection," she whispered.

"Is there anything else I should know about her?" Olivia asked, already bracing for an extensive list.

Jill's eyes brightened. "Oh, where do I even start?" She pulled out her phone, scrolling through what looked like a detailed list. "Her dietary needs are very specific. No grains, no artificial anything. I've brought her meals—organic, hand-prepared, of course. They're all labeled and in the fridge. Warm them up for two minutes in the microwave. I prefer them oven-warmed, but since there's no oven here, the microwave will have to do. Oh, and her water must be filtered and chilled—just not too cold. The fountain does most of that, but you know, just make sure it's perfect."

Olivia nodded, trying to keep her face neutral. "Got it. Warm meals, filtered water, and not too cold."

"And if it rains, wrap her in her special lavender-infused blanket," Jill added. "I've left it in the armoire in her room."

Olivia repeated the instructions under her breath, memorizing them. "Lavender blanket for storms. Got it."

Jill beamed. "Wonderful!" She reached into her bag and handed Olivia a manila folder. "Here's a list of everything we discussed, just in case you need it. There's an itinerary too—Chardonnay has duties, and she must be at the right place at the right time."

Olivia nodded, glancing at the folder. Jill gave her a flat stare. "I'm trusting you completely. Chardonnay is irreplaceable."

Before Olivia could respond, Jill's phone buzzed and she sighed. "Excuse me, the wedding planner is having another meltdown. I don't know why I hired all this 'help' when I seem to end up doing everything myself anyway, " she muttered.

With that, Jill turned and left, calling over her shoulder, "Remember, Olivia, nothing can go wrong with Chardonnay. Not a curl out of place."

As the door closed behind her, Olivia stood there for a moment, staring at the lavish room and the contented Chardonnay. She let out a breath and sank onto the couch. "Well, Elmer," she said out loud, knowing he could hear her from the other room. "This is going to be an interesting job. And we still have more four-legged guests to meet." From the bedroom she could hear Elmer snort, not thrilled with the idea of being encroached on by more pampered pets.

CHAPTER 4

Olivia barely had a moment to settle into the couch after Jill's grand exit before the next knock echoed through the room. She glanced down at Elmer, who had made his way into the living area, sighed dramatically and rested his chin on his paws. His eyes showing the resignation of a dog, aware that nap time was at risk.

"Probably our first guest," Olivia murmured, pushing herself off the couch. "I wonder who it is?"

Elmer didn't bother to lift his head as she crossed the living room to answer the door, abandoning any hope of peaceful sleep.

When Olivia opened the door, she was greeted by Shara, a bridesmaid she'd met earlier. Standing next to her was an immaculate blue-gray pit bull with a coat so glossy it gleamed in the sunlight. The dog moved with a quiet grace, though her expression was anything but thrilled.

"Olivia, right?" Shara asked, her voice carrying a note of polite urgency, as though her mind was occupied with a dozen other things. She had that air of someone who was running on fumes, barely keeping everything afloat. "I'm so sorry to do this, but Jill mentioned you're handling the pet-sitting for the wedding, and I... I need your help with Ayla.With the rehearsal dinner and the laundry list of things Jill wants me to take care of, I just can't give her the attention she deserves this weekend."

Olivia offered a warm smile. "Of course, come on in."

As Shara stepped inside, Ayla padded after her, the quiet sound of her paws on the floor betraying the elegance with which she carried herself. Elmer, ever the vigilant sentry, lifted his head slightly, giving the newcomer a careful once-over before determining she wasn't a threat. His gaze, however, flickered toward Chardonnay's room where the pampered pooch was lounging, and Olivia could tell he wasn't quite ready to share his territory with another dog of "that kind".

"Ayla's a sweetheart," Shara began, fumbling with the leash clasp, distracted. "But she... she has a very specific skincare routine that cannot slide."

Olivia blinked, her eyebrows furrowing in confusion. "Skincare routine?"

Shara sighed, as if the weight of her dog's dermatological needs had become a heavy burden. "She's prone to dryness so she needs to be moisturized twice a day—morning and night. It's really not a big deal, but with everything going on for the wedding, I just can't keep up with it. Jill said you'd be able to help," Shara added, her tone lifting with a hopeful edge.

"Moisturizing? Twice a day?" Olivia echoed, struggling to wrap her head around it.

Shara nodded, her face dead serious. "I know, it sounds a little ridiculous, but she loves it, and I can't skip it. Her vet recommended it and it has helped her, but if she gets off schedule, her skin dries out and it takes days to get her back to the proper moisture level. I've left all the products in her bag—there's a paw balm, a special cream for her nose, and a moisturizer for her belly. She also has a misting spray that should be used after each walk."

Olivia glanced down at Ayla, who was watching them with cool, patient eyes as if fully aware they were discussing her extensive self-care regimen. "Got it," Olivia said, her smile tight. "Creams, balms, moisturizers, and misting spray. No problem."

Shara exhaled in relief, her shoulders slumping. "You're a lifesaver. And if you could make sure she doesn't lick the lotion off right away, that would be great. Oh, and when she comes back inside from any walk, her paws need to be wiped—no matter what the weather's like. She hates dirt. Or mud. Or really, any form of uncleanliness."

Olivia turned to look at Elmer, who had taken up residence in a sunbeam, half-covered in dust he'd picked up after rolling around in the yard. He gave a lazy blink, totally unbothered by the concept of filth.

"Right," Olivia said, trying to muster enthusiasm despite her growing skepticism. "I'll make sure Ayla gets her beauty routine done exactly as needed."

Shara beamed, oblivious to Olivia's internal eye roll. "Jill said you were the right person for the job. I'll just leave her things by the door." She glanced down at Ayla, giving her an affectionate pat. "And one more thing—Ayla likes her bed fluffed every night. Extra cushy."

Olivia bit back a sigh. "Of course."

"She's also playing a special part in the wedding, so please make sure she's where she needs to be, on time. Jill gave you the itinerary, right? It lists all the events she needs to attend." Shara's tone was light, but the underlying urgency revealed the pressure Jill had placed on making sure everything—and everyone—was in the right place at the right time.

Olivia nodded toward the manila folder on the coffee table. "Yes, I have the itinerary."

"Fabulous!" Shara said brightly before handing Olivia the leash. With a final affectionate pat on Ayla's head, she hurried out the door, leaving Olivia alone with the dog.

The moment the door clicked shut, Olivia dropped onto the couch with a slow exhale, her shoulders sagging. She unclipped Ayla's leash, letting the dog roam around the room, taking in her new surroundings. Elmer gave a long, disapproving look at Ayla, then shifted his gaze to Olivia. She heard his thoughts loud and clear: *What have you gotten us into?* Olivia shook her head. "I don't know that I'm sure anymore, buddy."

Olivia ran a hand through her hair. "Hey, Elmer," she said, half-laughing. "Maybe we should set you up with a skincare routine, too." Elmer gave her a horrified look, as though she'd suggested he give up eating table scraps.

Ayla, unbothered, huffed softly before settling herself into one of the plush dog beds, crossing her paws as if settling in for a stay at a five-star resort. Elmer, ever the skeptic, watched her with a mix of amusement and judgment before collapsing back down with an exaggerated grunt.

Olivia pulled Ayla's bag over to inspect the contents. As she rifled through the assortment of lotions and creams, she paused when she came across the paw balm. The label featured an image of a serene, relaxed dog—one who had a more peaceful life than Olivia ever had. *This dog has more creams and lotions in one bag than I've had in my entire life,* Olivia thought, glancing at her own bag, which held the lone tube of lotion she'd packed for the weekend.

Ayla watched her closely, her gaze steady and expectant, as if waiting to see if Olivia would meet her lofty standards. Olivia sighed and checked the instructions left in the bag. "Guess we'll try this out before bed tonight," she muttered.

Before she had processed Ayla's full skincare regimen, a second knock sounded at the door.

"Here we go," Olivia muttered, tossing Ayla's instructions back into the bag.

From his sunspot, Elmer groaned; too many tasks, too many guests.

The knock came again, more insistent this time. Olivia sighed and crossed the room, bracing herself for whatever new chaos awaited her. She opened the door, expecting yet another pampered pooch, but instead found a tall, lanky man holding a silver crate. He looked like a deer caught in headlights, his nervousness evident.

"Uh, hi, Olivia," he said, his voice apologetic. "We met earlier. I'm Seth, and this," he raised the crate, "is Chester."

A low, disinterested meow came from inside the crate, followed by the unmistakable sound of a paw tapping against the side.

Olivia's eyebrows shot up. "Yes, I remember seeing him earlier—well, the leash that was supposedly attached to him," she said with a chuckle.

"Yeah, the leash thing is... interesting," Seth admitted with a grimace. "Jill insisted on it, and on him being part of the wedding. He's not a fan of the leash, or of traveling, or people, or dogs. Honestly, he's not a fan of much." He sighed deeply. "I didn't intend to include him. My usual sitter's booked, and all the boarding places around here are dealing with some kind of feline virus outbreak. I mentioned it to Jill weeks ago, and she 'saved the day' by finding him a spot here... so, well, here we are." The last part came out with a hint of sarcasm.

Olivia raised an eyebrow, her gaze shifting between Seth and Chester, who was glaring at her from inside the crate. The poor cat was visibly uncomfortable—his tail flicking nervously and his eyes darting around the unfamiliar surroundings.

"Jill's set on making sure everything is perfect for the pets, huh?" Olivia remarked, trying to keep the mood light as she knelt down to unlock the crate.

Seth gave a wry smile. "Yeah, 'perfect' is one word for it. The bridal party's less than thrilled with the whole animal-inclusion thing, and Desmond... well, he's not a fan of the whole 'pets at the wedding' idea either. He was okay with Chardonnay being involved because he knows how much she means to Jill, but as she kept adding more animals, his patience started wearing thin." He shrugged and glanced toward the room where Chardonnay lay napping. "But, y'know, Jill's got high expectations for everyone—pets included."

Olivia gave him a sympathetic smile as she let Chester out of the crate. The cat immediately skittered to the farthest corner of the room, clearly unsettled. "Sounds like she's got everyone on a tight leash," Olivia joked, though she noticed the subtle tension in Seth's voice.

"Yeah, well," Seth muttered, his hands slipping into his pockets, "she's the bride, and we're all just... along for the ride." Seth offered a weak smile. "Jill thought it would be better if Chester stayed here with you instead of with me. Apparently, some guests have cat allergies, and she didn't want me to get cat hair on my clothes and, you know, ruin the event." He rolled his eyes, then leaned in, lowering his voice. "Chester's got... an attitude. Just don't take it personally."

Olivia chuckled. "Well, don't worry. Chester will be in good hands." Seth glanced at the manila folder on the coffee table. "Oh, perfect, you have the itinerary." "His food's in here. And the leash.", he said, holding out a small bag. "Good luck with that—the trick to getting the harness on is to do it while he's distracted by something, usually food." Seth's eyes flicked to a little box in the far corner of the room. "And I see Jill made sure he's got all his... amenities. So he should be good to go." He glanced around the room once more and said, "Thanks, Olivia," as he turned to leave.

Olivia waved him off as she closed the door, looking down at Chester, who was still eyeing her. She couldn't help but smile at the irony—Jill had turned the entire event into a pet parade, but from the looks on the bridal party's faces, it wasn't exactly the wedding experience most of them had envisioned..

CHaPTer 5

A cheerful voice interrupted Olivia before she could close the door. "Oh, is this where we're leaving all the pets?" It was Katherine, another bridesmaid from earlier, balancing a birdcage precariously on her hip.

"This is Tulip," Katherine said with a proud smile, as if introducing her first-born. "You mentioned you're taking care of the pets, and Jill said I could drop her off with you." She paused for a moment, glancing down at the bird. "I'd love to take care of her myself, but well... Jill's got... expectations... that keep most of my time tied up until the wedding's over."

Olivia raised an eyebrow, sensing another bridal party member not thrilled with Jill's "expectations."

"Yes, I remember Tulip from her, uh, performance," Olivia said, trying to keep the conversation light. Katherine beamed, her smile widening.

"Doesn't she sing beautifully?" Katherine asked, before her smile faltered. "Well, not beautifully enough for Jill."

Inside the cage, a vibrant parrot fixed Olivia with a sharp, almost calculating gaze. "Hi there," it squawked, tilting its head. "How are you?"

Katherine glanced at the bird, giving a dismissive wave. "Tulip loves chatting. You can't get a word in with her. I've left a list of her favorite phrases and her feeding schedule in her bag. Just keep her away from the cats."

Olivia nodded. "Got it. And I assume her events are listed on the itinerary?"

Katherine nodded. "Yes, just make sure she's..."

"In the right place at the right time," Olivia finished for her. Katherine gave a tense smile, clearly eager to leave. "Exactly."

Tulip squawked again, piercing the stillness. "Pretty bird! Pretty bird!"

Katherine glanced at her petite gold watch, sighing. "Anyway, I need to go. Rehearsal dinner prep and all. Need to find that delightful bartender and grab another glass of champagne. Thanks so much!" With a quick wave, she was gone.

Olivia watched her leave, holding Tulip's cage and feeling an increasing sense of dread. The cracks in the bridal party's polished exterior were showing. None of them seemed thrilled about their pets being part of the wedding, yet they all seemed bound by Jill's overwhelming expectations. But her role was clear—keep the pets safe, fed, and on schedule, no matter what drama was brewing beneath the surface.

She glanced at Chester, who had claimed a spot under a bench by the window, his mood sour. Then at Ayla, who sat as poised as ever, and Elmer, who was staring at the growing zoo around him with palpable skepticism.

"Alright," Olivia muttered, setting Tulip's cage down on the counter. "We've got Chester the temperamental cat, Tulip the chatterbox, Ayla the skincare queen, and Elmer... well, at least you're on my side." She rubbed her temples, wondering how many more pets would show up before the night was over.

"Pretty bird!" Tulip squawked again.

Elmer groaned, burying his head between his paws.

Olivia barely had time to process the growing menagerie when the unmistakable sound of more paws approached the door. "Here we go again.," muttered Olivia, preparing herself for whoever was headed up the steps. She swung the door open, and before she could even greet the person on the other side, a small blur of brown fur bolted past her legs, barking up a storm.

"Benny! Benny, no!" the frazzled owner cried, rushing in after the darting dachshund.

Olivia watched in horror as the tiny, hyperactive dog zipped around the room like a tornado, barking non-stop, his little legs moving at lightning speed. Before she could stop him, Benny collided with the leg of a side table holding a decorative vase. The vase wobbled dangerously, tipping toward the edge. Acting quickly, Olivia lunged forward, catching it just before it hit the floor, steadying it with a sigh of relief.

Benny, of course, was oblivious, now attempting to wrestle a pillow off the couch, his tail wagging in a blur.

"I am so, so sorry!" Benny's owner, Rachel, Jill's other bridesmaid, practically tripped over herself as she tried to catch the dog. "He... uh, he has a lot of energy. I should've warned you."

"A lot of energy?" Olivia echoed, sidestepping as Benny tore past her again, nearly taking out another piece of furniture. "This dog's running on turbo mode!"

Rachel scooped Benny up, though it was more like wrestling with a squirming, over-caffeinated squirrel. Benny wriggled in her arms, barking excitedly at anything and everything. Olivia could almost see the static electricity bouncing off him.

"Benny, calm down!" Rachel pleaded, holding him close as he twisted his head to bark at a bird outside the window. "I swear, he's usually much better behaved."

Olivia raised an eyebrow, skeptical.

Rachel offered a sheepish smile. "Jill thought it'd be best if he stayed with you since... well, you've got experience with pets. and because I have a ton to do before the wedding. Leaving him alone in my cottage all day might be, well, disastrous."

Elmer lifted his head just in time to watch Benny wriggle out of Rachel's arms and dart under the couch.

Olivia could hear the tiny dachshund barking furiously at who-knows-what beneath the furniture.

"I'll... I'll get him out," Rachel stammered, crouching to reach for Benny. "I promise he'll calm down, eventually."

"Eventually," Olivia sighed, pinching the bridge of her nose. "Right."

Benny, of course, had no plans of calming down anytime soon. His barking continued from under the couch, muffled but no less loud, as his little paws scrabbled across the hardwood floor. Elmer, for his part, had given up entirely, lowering his head onto his paws with a long, suffering sigh.

"Pretty bird!" Tulip squawked from her cage, adding to the cacophony.

Olivia shot the parrot a warning glance. "Not helping, Tulip."

Tulip puffed out her chest. "Pretty bird! Woof!"

"Great, now she's imitating Benny," Olivia muttered, shaking her head as she crouched down to help Rachel coax the dachshund out. She peeked under the couch and saw Benny's wagging tail as he darted back and forth in the tight space, having the time of his life.

Rachel reached out for him, grabbing hold of his tiny collar. "Gotcha!" she exclaimed, pulling him out from under the couch with a victorious smile.

But Benny, not one to go down without a fight, started squirming again, barking at Tulip, who squawked back in what seemed like a taunt.

"Woof! Pretty bird! Woof!"

Olivia groaned, standing up and dusting herself off. "Okay, well, Benny's certainly... lively."

"That's one word for it," Rachel said, struggling to keep hold of him. "I'll, uh, leave his toys and things by the door. There is a list of care instructions in the bag. Just... good luck."

Before she left, Rachel turned back, her voice hesitant. "Oh, one more thing, Benny..."

"He has a part in the wedding," Olivia interjected, reciting the line with a knowing tone. "It's on the itinerary. He needs to be in the right place at the right time."

Rachel looked startled, but nodded. "Yes, exactly. Jill has..."

"Expectations," Olivia finished, her smile a little wry.

"You've obviously heard that one a time or two," Rachel remarked.

"One or two," Olivia replied with a grin.

"Well, okay then, I'm off," Rachel said, pushing through the door, visibly relieved to be free of her energetic, furry companion—at least for now.

The moment the door closed, Benny wasted no time resuming his frantic energy. He launched himself at a squeaky toy, shaking it like a wild animal, his tiny legs moving furiously.

Olivia stood for a moment, taking in the pandemonium unfolding around her. Between Benny's constant barking, Tulip's loud squawking, and Ayla's cool detachment from it all, the cottage was turning into something of a circus. Even Elmer, who usually stayed aloof from any sort of drama, had flattened his ears and was giving Olivia a look of pure dismay—one that screamed, *Is this really happening?*

"Well," Olivia sighed, rubbing her temples, "at least for the next couple of days. But we can handle it, right?" She glanced down at Elmer, whose eyes narrowed in response, skeptical of the idea of taking on any of this.

"At least I think we can handle it," Olivia muttered, glancing around as Benny zoomed past again, barely missing her foot.

Elmer gave her an exaggerated, world-weary look that said, *I'm not getting paid enough for this.*

"I know, buddy," Olivia sighed, staring at the mishmash of pets now under her care. "Neither am I."

She sank onto the floor with her back against the couch, exhaustion settling in. Reaching for the manila folder on the coffee table, she flipped it open to reveal the color-coded itinerary Jill had given her. Each pet had a corresponding color, and each event they were required to attend was highlighted with precision. Olivia blinked at the level of detail. *I've never seen a wedding with pre-parties for every event,* she thought. She knew weddings were a big deal, but this was something else. From the looks of it, tonight there was some kind of meet-and-greet in the gardens by the main house. Chardonnay was the only pet listed, but Olivia had already cleared with Jill that Elmer could accompany her to any of the events the other pets were invited to.

She glanced around the room. The pets seemed to be managing okay, at least for now. Benny had paused his manic zooming and was now circling the others, sniffing and greeting them one by one. Ayla, ever poised, greeted him politely, while Chester and Tulip eyed him with the wariness of animals who had no interest in interacting. Chardonnay, of course, couldn't be bothered to mingle with the others. She remained tucked in her room, resting on her luxurious bed like royalty. Elmer, ever watchful, lay on the floor, observing everything with cautious eyes.

Olivia sat back, her eyes scanning the room as she observed the collection of pets. She could sense their presence in her mind, a subtle pulse of energy that fluctuated depending on their moods—Benny's exuberance, Ayla's calm poise, Tulip's curiosity—but the thoughts themselves remained elusive. She had yet to fully tap into the animals' voices, which meant she could only feel their energy in the space between them and her.

It was a strange sort of awareness, like listening to static on the radio without catching the full signal. The animals were there, but their words weren't—yet.

If she could start hearing their thoughts, though, she knew it could get complicated. There was only so much room in her mind, and trying to juggle all their voices at once could send her into a dizzying spiral. She smiled wryly, imagining Benny's nonstop chatter mixed with

Tulip's sassy remarks, Ayla's dignified commentary, and Chester's aloof silence. It would be more than a little overwhelming.

For now, though, Olivia was thankful for the quiet. She knew it probably wouldn't stay that way.

Benny wandered over to Elmer, stretched out, and nestled into his side as though he'd found the perfect pillow. Elmer looked down at him, his expression a mix of confusion and reluctant acceptance. After a moment, he gave in, flopping onto his side with a resigned sigh. At least he'd get a nap out of it.

Olivia smiled at the unexpected sight. She felt a wave of relief wash over her, knowing that for now, at least, she wasn't breaking up animal fights or trying to separate everyone into corners. *Yet,* she reminded herself with a quiet chuckle. She hoped that if she fed everyone dinner and took them out for some exercise before the evening events, they'd settle in and behave while she was gone.

For the first time that day, the cottage seemed a little quieter—though that wasn't saying much.

CHAPTER 6

The sun dipped low on the horizon, casting a warm golden hue over Dogwood Cottage as Olivia stepped out of her guest cottage. Elmer trotted at her heels, his tail wagging in that perpetually hopeful way, while Chardonnay glided beside her with the grace of a true show dog, her glossy coat gleaming in the fading light. The evening buzzed with excitement, an energy that wrapped around the estate like an electric current. It was the start of the first official wedding event—a "meet and greet" that promised to be every bit the high-society cocktail party. The itinerary labeled the event "pets optional," a phrase Olivia wasn't sure she'd ever encountered before regarding a wedding. Of course, Chardonnay was never optional.

Olivia glanced over her shoulder at the other pets lounging in the cottage, contentedly curled up and unaware of the festive atmosphere outside. She figured if one of the other guests wanted their pets to accompany them, she could always go back and fetch them—but the vibe she'd picked up earlier told her she probably wouldn't need to.

As she made her way down the winding path that led to the sprawling gardens, the soft evening breeze carried the heady fragrance of blooming petals, mixed with faint laughter from the gathering ahead. Olivia's heart skipped a beat, a flutter of nerves rippling through her. She wasn't used to this world of wealth and sophistication. It was new, uncharted territory, and she was determined not to make any embarrassing mistakes—even though the guests seemed unconcerned about anything but their cocktails and canapes.

Upon arrival, the scene struck Olivia. Guests milled about under sprawling canopies of wisteria, their laughter ringing out like music, mingling effortlessly with the delicate glow of fairy lights twinkling overhead. Olivia couldn't help but admire the effortless elegance surrounding her. She spotted Jill glowing with joy as she effortlessly charmed everyone within earshot. As Olivia made her way over with Elmer and Chardonnay in tow, Jill's eyes lit up at the sight of her dog.

"There's my girl!" Jill exclaimed, bending down to lavish Chardonnay with attention, as if she had just returned from an extended absence rather than spending the day apart. Turning to the gathered crowd, Jill beamed. "Here is the real star of the show, ladies and gentlemen!"

she announced, her voice carrying over the hum of conversation. A ripple of polite laughter spread through the crowd, as if they were all in on the joke. Chardonnay, ever the obedient diva, hopped onto a small platform nearby, designed for this special moment in the spotlight. A plush cushion awaited her, and she circled it a few times before lying down, surveying the scene with an air of regal contentment. Olivia couldn't help but smile at the sight. Chardonnay, in all her glory, was in her element, basking in the attention like the seasoned show dog she was.

Olivia's mouth curved into a smile; she muttered, "Lucky girl." Elmer, ever the enthusiast, sniffed the air as though he were about to discover a hidden treasure. He looked up at Olivia, tail wagging, and she nudged him gently. "Best manners, right?"

Elmer stayed close to Olivia, but she could see the excitement bubbling in him. His ears perked up as he glanced around, aware of the crowd's energy. He was calculating, weighing how much attention and affection he could garner now that Chardonnay was nearby. His tail gave a few tentative wags, as if plotting when to make his move, but for now, he stayed by Olivia.

As Olivia moved deeper into the festivities, she couldn't help but observe the mood of the crowd. Many of the guests were genuinely enjoying themselves, laughing and chatting as they indulged in the lavish spread that was laid out for the evening. But others seemed to play a part, their enjoyment more forced than authentic. They had the air of actors, placed in the scene to fill out the picture, not to truly be part of it. *Maybe this is how high society works,* Olivia thought. Maybe acquaintances and so-called friends attend for status, career, or other unspoken reasons, rather than to celebrate the couple and share in their happiness.

Olivia passed by a group of chatting women led by Katherine, talking animatedly. She had a drink in hand and was laughing lightly, but her words carried an edge.

"I mean, honestly, Jill's obsession with Chardonnay is just ridiculous," Katherine said, shaking her head as she glanced around, keeping her voice low. "If she really wanted to make animals a part of the wedding, she should've chosen ones with actual talent. Like Tulip, for example. That bird can sing—not just prance around looking pretty."

Katherine smirked, pleased with her own assessment. "I mean, a dog in a wedding? Fine, but it's not like they're doing anything special. Tulip, on the other hand—she's a star. She's got the skills, and let's be honest, everyone knows it." She took a sip of her drink, reveling in her own words.

Olivia's brow furrowed as she listened to the conversation. The dismissiveness in Katherine's tone made her uneasy. She had mentioned Tulip not getting enough attention before, but the way she spoke now hinted at something deeper—jealousy. Katherine wasn't just frustrated; she was envious, perhaps feeling overlooked in favor of Chardonnay.

Flowing dresses swayed in the breeze, and clusters of men in tailored suits stood in groups, drinks in hand, chatting and laughing. The mood was light, but her attention was drawn elsewhere—toward Monica, the groom's sister. Monica was flitting through the crowd like a butterfly, effortlessly engaging everyone in conversation with a practiced charm that didn't seem genuine. Her laughter was high-pitched, but Olivia sensed something hollow behind it. She watched as Monica laughed with the women, discussing designer handbags, while also lightly touching the arms of the surrounding men, a flirtatious touch here and there, as if weaving a web of attention around herself.

Meanwhile, Desmond—Jill's fiancé—stood off to the side, his posture stiff, his eyes darting around the crowd. A stark contrast to the carefree festivities, Desmond fidgeted, throwing anxious glances toward the others. Olivia couldn't help but notice the sharp, loaded exchanges between Monica and Desmond, their interactions increasingly tense and fraught. At one point, when Monica had joined Desmond and a few other men to chat, she had leaned in close to Desmond, whispering something that made him stiffen, his lips pressing into a tight line. He gave a curt nod, but his body language screamed discomfort—his hand shifted nervously to adjust his tie, and his eyes flickered to the ground, avoiding her gaze. Monica's response was a stiff smile, her fingers lingering a little too long on his arm as she pulled away, clearly enjoying the moment of control. The silence between them stretched, charged with something unspoken, before Desmond exhaled, forcing a tight smile and redirecting his attention to the crowd.

Olivia, who had been watching from a distance, couldn't shake the feeling that their conversation had been more than just sibling banter—it was a silent battle of wills. Something wasn't right between them, and it had nothing to do with the wedding. The exchange seemed to hold deeper layers, the tension between them thick enough for Olivia to feel it even from across the garden. *What was really going on between the groom and his sister? And why did Desmond look so uneasy around her?*

She noticed a rustic gazebo, ivy-covered and twinkling with fairy lights, at the garden's edge. A small wooden sign displaying the words "Tarot Readings" nailed to the outside. "Come on, Elmer! Let's see what Mom is up to," Olivia said, pushing aside the weight of the suspicions still nagging at her mind.

"Let's see what the universe has in store for you tonight!" Olivia's mother, Cassandra, called out, her voice filling the air with a mystical charm as she shuffled a deck of tarot cards in front of a young couple, their fingers intertwined and faces flushed from the wine they'd shared. Olivia felt a surge of pride for her mother, whose ability to engage and enchant was a well-known gift in Emerald Ridge.

Just then, one guest burst out laughing, exclaiming, "I think I only want a reading about my stock portfolio!" The group erupted in laughter, and Olivia's gaze shifted to Elmer, who had come to a complete stop, his nose twitching as the smells from a nearby hors d'oeuvres table floated by on a breeze. His tail wagged excitedly, as if he had stumbled upon a gourmet meal.

"Not everything is a snack for you, you know," Olivia teased, but Elmer, with his unwavering focus on the delicacies laid out, had other plans. "Not tonight, pastry bandit!" she warned, tugging gently on his collar as he sidled closer to the delicious smells.

Monica's laughter rang out again, cutting through the festivities like a sharp note in an otherwise harmonious melody. At the sound of Monica's laughter. a group of women nearby exchanged sharp glances, their heads tilting ever so slightly, as if discussing something not meant for public ears. Intrigued, Olivia moved closer, hoping to catch a snippet of conversation.

"Did you hear about Monica's latest investment?" one woman whispered, her voice tinged with both excitement and caution. "It could either make her or break her—it's all anyone's talking about."

Olivia's pulse quickened. She knew little about Monica beyond what Jill had shared, but it was becoming clear there were layers to her behavior that Olivia hadn't fully grasped. The subtle whispers, the calculated way Monica seemed to command attention—it was as if there was something she was hiding behind her showy charm. Olivia's suspicion deepened. Monica's over-the-top actions, paired with the undercurrents of tension with Desmond, suggested there was far more beneath the surface than anyone was letting on. Something about her didn't sit right, and Olivia could feel it growing harder to ignore.

As the evening unfolded, the laughter and elegance of the wedding surrounded Olivia, but the questions still lingered in the air, unanswered. Her gaze drifted across the garden, taking in the beauty that masked the secrets it held. The more she observed, the stronger the pull became—there was more to this night, more to the people and the whispers, and she had a role to play in it, whether or not she was ready. She couldn't shake the memory of the last time her instincts had told her something wasn't quite right—and how that had led her down a path with far more layers to uncover than she'd ever expected.

As the evening wound down, Olivia felt the energy of the party seep out of her, leaving her with a deep sense of fatigue. "We should get back to the cottage and check on the others," Olivia said to Elmer. Though the lack of snacks disappointed him, Elmer seemed ready to return to the quiet of their little cottage.

Just then, Jill appeared at her side, holding out Chardonnay's leash with a bright, expectant smile.

"Thank you so much for taking care of her, Olivia. I'll sleep much better tonight knowing she's in such capable hands. Now, you better get back to the cottage. My girl needs her beauty sleep." With one last pat on Chardonnay's head, Jill handed her over to Olivia and hurried off to rejoin Desmond by the bar.

"Let's go check in with Mom before we head back," Olivia said to the dogs, giving Chardonnay a reassuring smile as they made their way toward her mother's tarot station.

Cassandra was mid-reading when Olivia arrived; her guest looked increasingly bewildered as Cassandra laid out the cards. "Ah! The Moon!" Cassandra exclaimed dramatically, her fingers trailing over the cards. "Illusions abound! Beware of false friends!"

The guest, a young woman with a flushed face, rose quickly, shaking her head. "I think I've had enough of the universe for tonight," she muttered, her voice uncertain. As she left, Olivia slipped into the now-vacant chair opposite her mother. "Hey, Mom! Just wanted to check in before we head back to the cottage," she said, gesturing to Elmer and Chardonnay, who had flopped down beside her.

Cassandra stood to give her a quick hug, but her expression shifted, her voice dropping to a conspiratorial whisper. "I've been picking up some strange energy tonight, Liv. It's all a bit off. Every reading I've done has had an odd undercurrent. But there was something especially strange when I read for Katherine—I think she's a bridesmaid? Her energy was... tangled, like she's hiding something, or maybe just caught in something she doesn't fully understand herself."

Olivia frowned, curiosity piqued. "Katherine, huh? That's unsettling."

Her mother's eyes grew distant, scanning the crowd. "There's something going on here that's deeper than any of them realize. Keep an eye on Monica, too. She's tangled in secrets, and not just hers..."

Before Olivia could respond, another guest approached the table, eager to hear their fortune. Cassandra gave Olivia a knowing look, cutting their conversation short. The air felt heavier now, and Olivia couldn't shake the feeling that her mother's instincts were more than just a hunch.

Olivia said goodbye to her mother, then walked back towards the cottage, her mind buzzing with her mother's revelations. The night air had cooled, the sounds of laughter and music fading as she walked. The questions lingered, unanswered, but one thing was clear: there was far more at play here. She just wasn't sure what yet.

CHAPTER 7

Olivia's morning started abruptly, her peaceful sleep shattered by Elmer's low growl—a deep, rumbling sound that echoed through the quiet cottage like distant thunder. She blinked against the soft, golden light filtering through the windows and sat up groggily. The stillness felt wrong, a heavy silence that set alarm bells ringing in her mind. By this time, she would assume the pets would be shuffling around the cottage, nails clicking on the hardwood in a predictable rhythm, waiting impatiently for breakfast. But she hadn't heard any annoyed barks or been prodded by any wet noses. But today? Nothing. An unsettling silence hung over the cottage.

Olivia walked to the door of the bedroom and glanced out in the main area of the cottage, scanning the room, her gaze falling on the other animals. They were all fast asleep, blissfully unaware of the growing tension in the air. But something was amiss. She noticed the door to Chardonnay's room was ajar; the hinges creaking with a faint squeak, as if the door had been moved recently.

That's strange, she thought. *I'm sure I closed it last night.*

A creeping sense of dread slowly spread through Olivia as she approached Chardonnay's door. Her heart quickened with each step. When she pushed the door open, the sight that met her made her stomach drop. The dog bed lay empty, though rumpled blankets hinted Chardonnay had slept there. A tightness gripped Olivia's chest. *Could she have just wandered off?*

Standing in the doorway, Olivia's mind raced back to the night before. She remembered bringing Chardonnay back to the cottage, settling her into the room, and closing the door behind her. She recalled turning on the tiara-shaped nightlight that Jill had placed on the nightstand—Chardonnay didn't like to sleep in complete darkness. Olivia turned slowly in a tight circle, taking in every detail of the room, trying to make sense of what had happened. The cottage doors were closed, the windows locked. She couldn't just vanish into thin air, could she? So where had Chardonnay gone?

Elmer poked his head around the door, wondering where Olivia had gone. She turned to him, her voice soft.

"Elmer," she whispered, calling her four-legged companion. "Where's Chardonnay?"

Elmer padded over to her and sat down, curious about what she was looking at in the empty room. But as soon as he sniffed the air, his expression shifted. His gaze flicked from the empty bed to Olivia, and she could hear his thoughts loud and clear. *Chardonnay. Gone.*

"I know, but gone where?," Olivia muttered, panic seeping into her words. This wasn't good.

Frantically, she moved through the cottage, checking behind furniture and under tables. Desperation made her thorough, even though she knew Chardonnay couldn't possibly be hiding in any of these places. The bathroom door creaked open to reveal—nothing. A sinking feeling took root in her stomach. *Where could she be?*

Olivia stepped back into Chardonnay's room, her mind racing as her eyes swept over the space once more. The empty bed taunted her. The water bowl sat untouched, an eerie reminder that the dog had been there, but not anymore. A sense of unease crawled up her spine, her instincts prickling. Something was off.

She had been so sure everything was in order last night—she'd secured Chardonnay in her room, double-checked the other pets, and then retired to the second bedroom for the night. But now, with Chardonnay gone, her confidence was unraveling. *Had she really closed the door behind her?* The question gnawed at her.

Her pulse quickened as she stepped further into the room, the silence wrapping around her. Her hand brushed along the smooth edge of the doorframe, and she let her gaze linger on every detail again, hoping something would stand out. Maybe there was something she had missed—a

clue, an indication of what had happened. But all she saw
was the same empty space,

Then something strange caught her attention. A faint,
chilly breeze brushed past her legs, raising the hairs on
the back of her neck. Olivia froze, her breath catching in
her throat. Her senses, already on edge, snapped into high
alert. The source of the cold draft, a cracked sliding door,
drew her attention. The gap was small, but wide enough
for a hand—or a paw—to slip through.

She blinked, her stomach sinking. The door had
definitely been closed last night. She remembered it
clearly—locking it behind her after checking on all the
pets, the satisfying click of the latch. But now, uncertainty
crept in. *Had she missed something? Or had someone
tampered with the door?* Her fingers hovered near the lock,
but before she could touch it, doubt took root. The weight
of the room seemed to press in on her, her thoughts
spinning—caught between the growing unease and the
tight knot of tension in her chest.

No, she thought, trying to steady her breath, *this can't be
happening. It must be a mistake. A draft, maybe.* But the
air felt colder now, a subtle chill that made her skin prickle
with unease. She kneeled down, inspecting the door more
closely, her fingers tracing the edge of the frame. The metal
track was cold beneath her touch, and the breeze still crept
through, unsettling in its persistence. It seemed impossible
that Chardonnay could have left the cottage on her own,
but she had to check—just to be sure.

"Come on, Elmer," she called, the dog's presence a small comfort in the growing tension. "We're going to look for Chardonnay."

Without hesitation, Elmer bounded toward the door, eager for the search to begin. The moment Olivia opened it, he rushed out, his paws tapping lightly against the floorboards as if he already knew what was at stake.

They stepped outside into the morning air, which was already beginning to warm as the sun climbed higher in the sky. Olivia scanned the grounds around the cottage, the quiet of the morning amplifying the weight in her chest. Elmer immediately set to work, his nose twitching as he sniffed every inch of the yard, picking up the faintest scents carried by the breeze.

"Elmer, where is she?" Olivia murmured, squinting against the brightness of the sun as she moved toward the side of the cottage. Her eyes swept over the small patch of grass behind the building and the dense trees lining the edge of the property. Sweat trickled down her back, her thoughts a blur. She couldn't tell if the dampness on her skin was from the rising heat or her growing panic.

Elmer sniffed a patch of grass near the back door, his nose working diligently as he sifted through the smells of the yard. Olivia's eyes followed him as he moved through the yard, weaving around flower beds. The silence of the morning interrupted only by the occasional rustling of leaves.

As Olivia trailed Elmer around the cottage, her gaze caught something just off to the side. It was green, vine-like, and unmistakably familiar. Her stomach dropped as her eyes locked on the poison ivy. Its three-pointed leaves, glossy and dangerous, wound their way along the foundation of the cottage, tangled in the wildflowers. Elmer, already moving closer, seemed unaware of the threat. Olivia's heart raced as she rushed toward him, grabbing his collar just as he stepped closer.

"Elmer, no!" she exclaimed, her voice tight with urgency.

He gave a startled bark, halting in his tracks and looking up at her with confusion. Olivia let out a shaky breath, feeling her pulse quicken. She glanced down at her own arms, realizing how close she had come to brushing against the toxic plants. The last thing either of them needed was a run-in with poison ivy.

"Stay away from that," Olivia muttered, leading him a few steps back, scanning the ground for any signs of Chardonnay. She felt her frustration rise. *Where are you, girl?*

The quiet of the morning felt heavier now, as if the world itself was holding its breath. Olivia scanned her surroundings, taking in the stillness—the absence of chirping birds or rustling critters in the underbrush. All that filled the air was the hum of the wind through the trees.

She swept her gaze over the area once more, searching for any sign of movement, any trace of Chardonnay's distinctive paw prints or her shiny coat glinting in the sunlight. But there was nothing.

As they continued their search, Olivia couldn't shake the growing tension inside her. If Chardonnay didn't turn up soon, she'd have to tell Jill. And that was something she really didn't want to do.

Kneeling down, Olivia gave Elmer a quick scratch behind the ears, her voice low and earnest. "Find her, boy. Find Chardonnay."

Elmer paused, sniffing the earth beneath his paws, his focus sharp as he worked his way along the ground. Olivia's eyes scanned the yard again, hoping for any sign of movement, but everything remained still. She climbed the back porch steps, her mind racing, as Elmer continued to circle the treeline.

Approaching the sliding door, Olivia ran her hands along the edge of the track, feeling for anything out of the ordinary. "Ouch!" she yelped, pulling her hand back. She looked down and saw a small cut bleeding on her palm. Glancing closer at the door, she noticed the track was rough, dented in places, as though something had been used to pry it open. Her heart skipped a beat as she bent closer to inspect the door more closely. Faint smudges marked the glass—*dirty handprints? Or possibly fingerprints?* The thought made her stomach tighten.

Her pulse quickened as she turned to call Elmer back to her side, but before she could, a glint of something in the sunlight caught her attention. She froze, her breath catching in her chest. There, just beside the bottom step, lay Chardonnay's rhinestone collar, gleaming like a precious gem. Beside it was her favorite toy, caked in mud and looking out of place, as if it had been dragged through the dirt. Olivia's heart raced, realization sinking in. *This wasn't just a dog wandering off. This was deliberate.*

Elmer trotted over, sniffing at the collar and toy, sensing the change in Olivia's demeanor. She stood frozen, trying to process the unsettling turn of events.

"Elmer," Olivia said, her voice now low and tense. "Did you hear something earlier? Is that why you growled?"

Elmer blinked, his head tilting slightly as he thought. Olivia caught the flash of his response in her mind. *Footsteps. Noises. Didn't like it.*

"You should have woken me up!" Olivia snapped, running her fingers through her tangled hair. Elmer's response was calm and unapologetic. *I hear things you don't. Not all of them are important.*

Olivia's breath caught in her throat. *How had someone gotten into the cottage so silently?* She replayed the events of the night before, trying to recall any small sound that might have signaled a disturbance. *Was she too distracted? Had she let her guard down?*

Olivia's mind raced as she inspected the toy. The toy was freshly muddied; that wouldn't happen at night unless it had been outside.

"Who would do this?" she whispered to herself, her voice tinged with disbelief.

Elmer nudged her with his snout. His eyes were full of concern, and his thoughts, as usual, were clear. *We'll find her*, he reassured her, though the uncertainty in his expression told Olivia there were still many questions left unanswered.

"Chardonnay is gone, Elmer. We have to tell Jill," Olivia said, her voice grim. The realization of what she'd have to explain—of what had happened—settled like a weight in her chest.

Elmer's gaze turned to the door, then back to Olivia. *This is gonna be bad.*

CHaPTer 8

Olivia dashed toward the main house, her heart pounding in her chest. Elmer followed close behind, his tail low, ears pinned flat against his head, as if he, too, sensed the gravity of the situation. Inside, the house buzzed with the chaotic energy of last-minute wedding preparations, but it only made the tension in Olivia's chest tighten. Jill, surrounded by color-coded charts and floral arrangements in various stages of completion, was caught in the frenzy of wedding-day panic.

Olivia's voice strained, but steady, called out to her.

Jill looked up, face flush with the frantic energy of a bride trying to manage a million details at once. But the moment her eyes met Olivia's, the air seemed to shift. The gleam of excitement in Jill's eyes flickered and died, replaced by a spark of something darker—something that made her entire posture tighten.

"What's wrong?" Jill asked, her voice faltering, a crack in the facade of her calm composure. "You look like you've seen a ghost."

Olivia inhaled, forcing herself to hold it together, but her hands were shaking. "It's Chardonnay... She's missing."

Jill's face drained of color, her breath catching in her throat. Her hands, which had been deftly arranging napkins, froze, the sudden tremble in her fingers betraying the sheer panic that erupted within her. "What do you mean, missing?" Her voice was too high, too tight.

"I woke up this morning, and she wasn't in the cottage," Olivia said, her voice level despite the rising storm in her chest. "The patio door was open, and I found her collar and one of her toys outside."

Jill's lips parted, her entire body going rigid. Her hands gripped the edge of the table, knuckles turning white as she leaned forward, her voice barely a whisper. "How does a dog just disappear like that? In the middle of all this? You were with her all night, weren't you?"

Olivia swallowed, the truth of the situation pressing heavily against her lungs. "Yes, I was there all night. But the cottage was silent—completely silent—and none of the other pets made a sound. I didn't hear anything."

Jill's gaze darted around the room, her eyes wild, searching for something—anything—that could make sense of this. "Do you think someone… took her? Someone did this?" she asked, the words leaving her mouth in a frantic rush.

"I'm not sure," Olivia replied, trying to steady her nerves. "But I need to know if you've noticed anything strange—anything at all—that could help."

Jill's hands flew to her face, the desperation and fear washing over her like a tidal wave. "I—I can't think of anything… but you have to find her, Olivia!" Her voice cracked, a sob breaking free before she could stop it. Jill sank into a chair, her face crumpling as her hands covered her face. "Chardonnay's the most important part of this wedding! She has to be here!"

Olivia's heart twisted at the sight of Jill's anguish. Despite everything, despite the drama of the wedding, this was the moment that truly mattered to Jill. Chardonnay was the centerpiece, the queen of the day, and her absence was a crack in the foundation of the entire event.

"I will," Olivia promised, kneeling in front of Jill, her voice low but firm. "I'll find her. But I need you to stay calm. Let me handle this."

Jill's tear-filled eyes met hers, and for a moment, the façade of the perfect bride shattered. "Please, Olivia," she whispered, her voice breaking, "you have to bring her back."

Jill stood up from her chair, her face pale and strained, the weight of her fear settling over her like a storm cloud. She clutched the back of the chair for support, her breath shallow, hands trembling. "Everyone!" she cried, her voice high-pitched, frantic. "Stop what you're doing! Chardonnay has gone missing and we need to find her-now!"

A few people glanced up, startled by the sudden outburst, but the panic in Jill's eyes left no room for hesitation. She spun toward the staff, her voice rising as the gravity of the situation gripped her. "I need everyone—NOW!" she shouted, and there was no mistaking the urgency in her tone. "Check the entire property. The gardens, the woods, the grounds—all of it! We need to find her."

The room fell into a stunned silence before chaos erupted. One assistant dropped the floral arrangements she'd been fussing over, and another rushed to grab the wedding planner's radio. Rachel and Shara, two of the bridesmaids, exchanged glances, their faces pale as they scrambled to follow Jill's orders. The staff moved with newfound purpose, scattering in every direction, each person driven by Jill's commanding desperation.

Jill, her chest heaving with ragged breaths, turned back to Olivia, her eyes wide, wet with tears. "I can't do this without her, Olivia," she whispered, her voice cracking under the pressure. "Chardonnay has to be here. She's everything. If she's not here, nothing matters."

Olivia nodded, trying to suppress the rising tide of anxiety in her own chest. "We'll find her, Jill. We will." But the raw panic in Jill's voice made Olivia wonder if the frantic search might not be about just a missing dog—if it might be something more.

Jill's panic only intensified as she paced back and forth, wringing her hands. "Where could she be? She couldn't have just disappeared!" Her voice wavered with every step. She paused, her eyes darting around the room, as if expecting Chardonnay to magically appear.

Jill paused, pulled out her phone, tapping the screen with urgency. As the phone rang, her gaze darted to Olivia, a mixture of frustration and desperation on her face. "I need to report a missing dog," Jill's voice trembled through the speakerphone. "It's my poodle, Chardonnay. She's gone missing, and I need help to find her."

Olivia, still standing nearby, could hear every word, the tension in Jill's voice making her stomach tighten.

The dispatcher's voice, calm and detached, came through the phone. "I understand, ma'am. We'll send someone out to assist you. Stay where you are and don't leave the area."

"Yes, yes, just please hurry!" Jill's voice cracked with the plea. She tossed the phone onto the table and resumed her restless pacing. Olivia could hear her shallow breaths, the panic gnawing at her. Olivia knew that calling the police was a desperate measure and even if they hurried, which wasn't likely in this situation, they still wouldn't be there quick enough for Jill.

After what felt like an eternity, the sound of tires crunching on gravel reached her ears. Jill bolted toward the door, throwing it open just as two officers stepped out of their patrol car. One was tall and broad-shouldered, the other shorter, with a more reserved demeanor. Jill's eyes widened as she stepped toward them, her words rushing out. "What took you so long?" she demanded, her tone sharp with mounting anxiety.

The officers exchanged a brief, bewildered glance, but said nothing.

"Ma'am, we're here to help," the taller officer said, his voice steady but lacking any actual sense of urgency.

Jill frantically motioned for them to come inside. "Please, you have to help me! Chardonnay's missing. She's not just any dog. She's a show dog—champion bloodlines, worth a fortune. Chardonnay is irreplaceable. This is... this is serious!" Her voice cracked on the last word, a mix of frustration and fear.

The officer raised an eyebrow, taking in her frantic demeanor. He cleared his throat, his tone turning more practical. "Ma'am, we're not really set up to search for missing pets. We handle emergencies, not lost animals."

Jill froze, her eyes widening in disbelief. "No, no, you don't understand! Chardonnay... she's everything! She's the centerpiece of this wedding—my happiness. Without her, I—" Her voice trembled for a moment, but she quickly regained control, shifting her tone to something more urgent and calculating. "She's an incredibly valuable asset—worth thousands on the black market. I can't stress enough how important she is."

The officers exchanged a look, unsure how to respond to the mention of the black market. The smaller officer, who had remained silent until now, stepped forward, his tone more direct. "We'll take down the information, ma'am. But I need to make sure you understand—we don't typically handle pet searches. If you have specific areas you want us to focus on, we can help, but it's the owner's responsibility to search for a lost pet. You'll need to contact animal services or a specialized search team for anything more... suited to your situation."

Jill's shoulders slumped in defeat as the officers finished taking down the details. They exchanged final pleasantries, then turned to leave. Once the door shut behind them, Jill remained still, staring at the ground for a moment before glancing back at Olivia, as though realizing she was still there.

Her voice was quieter now, raw with emotion. "What do I do now?" she asked, her gaze searching Olivia's face for answers.

Olivia could see the shift that had happened within her—half the wedding preparations were still in motion, but her heart wasn't in any of it. It wasn't about the ceremony anymore. It was about Chardonnay.

Jill's voice cracked as she spoke. "I can't believe this is happening."

Olivia took a deep breath, trying to calm the unease in her chest. "We'll find her, Jill. I'll do everything I can. We just need to keep looking."

Jill didn't seem to hear her. Her gaze instead rested on the wedding assistants across the room. She hurried over to them, her voice rising with urgency. "Get everything finished up. The food, the seating—just keep it running. I have to go find my dog."

The assistant nodded, her expression a mix of confusion and concern. "Jill, are you sure you—"

"I'm sure," Jill snapped, her voice trembling. "She's not just a dog—she's like my child. I have to find her. I'll be back as soon as I can. I swear, if anything happens to her..." Her voice broke, and she spun away, her eyes flashing with panic as she rushed out the door.

As Jill dashed out the door, Olivia felt a knot tighten in her stomach. Outside the windows, she saw people clambering across the lawn, crossing paths, shouting to one another as they searched. More people had been called in to help. The wild, frantic scramble of the search had swept up the bridesmaids, groomsmen, and any available guests.

Olivia couldn't keep still. She turned back to Elmer, whose ears were perked up as he tried to make sense of the situation. They both knew the weight of what was happening, but there was little they could do but keep looking. Time was slipping through their fingers.

CHapTer 9

Olivia rushed out behind Jill, her eyes scanning the chaotic scene unfolding across the estate. People were darting in every direction, calling for Chardonnay, their voices cutting through the stillness of the morning. The air felt thick with tension, all the wedding preparations coming to a standstill. Every person out there seemed invested in the search, and Olivia could feel the weight of the situation pressing down on her. Chardonnay was more than just a dog—she was the heart of the event, and her disappearance was shaking the foundation of everything. The tension had permeated through the crowd; no one could ignore how much Chardonnay meant to Jill, or how her absence threatened to unravel all the carefully laid plans.

Olivia spotted Monica at the far end of the lawn, walking between the trees, but something about her caught Olivia's attention. Monica wasn't really searching for Chardonnay. Instead, she kept glancing over her shoulder, her posture stiff and distracted, as if her efforts were more about going through the motions than engaging in the search. Olivia watched as Monica moved with a sense of detached urgency, but it was clear she wasn't paying attention to the ground or even the surrounding people. In fact, Monica was engrossed in her phone, her thumb swiping across the screen. Monica's attempt to search was more about appearances than actual effort to find the missing dog.

Near the hedges, Katherine paced, showing little more interest in the search than Monica. Olivia noticed Katherine wringing her hands, her wide eyes scanning the area with a tense, almost paranoid energy. It was as if everyone else searching for Chardonnay was a potential threat. Her gaze flicked back and forth between the people on the lawn and the nearby woods, as though something—or someone—out there was unsettling her. What had started as frantic energy now felt more uncomfortable, tinged with impatience and suspicion. Katherine checked the same spots, as if expecting something to change or perhaps unsure of where else to look.

Olivia's stomach twisted as she watched the chaos unfold. It was clear that some people were more invested in finding Chardonnay than others were.

Turning away from the frantic search, Olivia knew she had done all she could for now. There was more to this than just a missing dog—she needed to find clues, and she needed to do it now. She called to Elmer, who trotted over, and together, they made their way back to the pet cottage.

The gravel path crunched beneath Olivia's boots as she approached the cottage, Elmer padding behind her. Her mind buzzed with questions about Chardonnay's disappearance—*where could she be? Who would take her? And why?* She turned the questions over in her mind, searching for something she might have missed.

As she reached the back patio, something faint caught her eye—barely visible against the dirt near the edge of the flowerbed. Kneeling down, her breath caught in her throat as she saw it clearly. A small, muddy paw print.

"Interesting," Olivia muttered, her fingers hovering just above the print without touching it. It wasn't much, but it was enough to make her pulse quicken. From its size, shape, and depth, she was sure it belonged to a dog, not a wild animal. The print seemed too deliberate, too purposeful. She hadn't taken any of the other pets outside the back of the cottage, and the print was too small to be Elmer's. Plus, it looked fresh—morning dew had preserved it, which meant it had to have happened before dawn. It appeared as if a dog had been led away from the cottage.

Looking closer, Olivia noticed a few divots in the dirt around the paw print, as though someone—or something—had been digging their feet into the ground, trying to resist being pulled away.

Elmer trotted up beside her, sniffing the print with interest, before looking back at Olivia. His gaze was focused, his thoughts clear: *Chardonnay.*

Olivia pulled out her phone to take a picture of the print. It wasn't solid evidence, but it was something—a tangible clue. The collar, the toy, the open door, and now this. She knew they were all pieces of the same puzzle, but how did they all fit together?

Standing, Olivia turned back toward the cottage, wishing she had stopped at Ashley's coffee bar before coming back. A good cup of coffee wouldn't bring Chardonnay back, but it might have eased her nerves.

As she entered the cottage, she mentally reviewed what she knew so far. *The collar near the back steps, the toy left behind, the paw print.* Someone had taken Chardonnay. But the real question was, why?

Olivia's thoughts were interrupted when Chester, the large Persian cat, ambled over to her. He stopped in front of Olivia and fixed her with a steady, unblinking gaze, as if waiting for something.

Someone was here. Chester's voice echoed in Olivia's mind. *In the dark. Bare feet.*

"Bare feet?" Olivia repeated, startled by the clarity of the message. "And when you woke up, Chardonnay was gone?"

Chester blinked slowly, his tail swishing, as if weighing whether to offer more information.

The idea of someone being barefoot seemed odd, especially since the cottage was far removed from the main wedding activities. Whoever had been here had been careful—silent, deliberate. They hadn't wandered in by accident; it was purposeful. They hadn't wanted the sound of shoes to give them away.

She glanced down at Elmer, who was sitting at her feet, watching her with his usual quiet intelligence.

"We've got work to do, buddy," she said.

Just as she turned to leave the cottage, something caught her eye. She looked toward the window and saw Monica standing alone at the top of the path leading to the guest accommodations. With her back turned to the crowd, she was talking on the phone, having abandoned the search for Chardonnay.

Olivia's skin prickled with unease. Something about Monica didn't sit right with her. *Shouldn't the maid of honor be at the heart of the wedding preparations? Shouldn't she be just as concerned about the bride's missing dog as Jill was?* But Monica? She was always glued to her phone, never fully present. And now, her behavior seemed even more elusive, more secretive than before.

Chardonnay's disappearance was no accident. Olivia was sure of that. But finding out who was involved—and why—was another matter entirely.

As time passed, many of those who had initially joined the frantic search for Chardonnay had quietly given up. The grounds, once bustling with people calling for the dog, had grown quiet. The few still searching moved more slowly now, their efforts marked by weariness, as if hope had faded.

By the time the early morning search wound down, the wedding guests had dispersed for the afternoon, with no events planned until the evening. Jill had arranged tours and hikes, allowing everyone the freedom to explore the property. Most of the guests seemed to embrace the quiet solitude the expansive estate provided.

Olivia settled the pets for the day before leashing Elmer and heading toward the woods. She needed time to think, to search for anything else that might help her unravel the mystery—another stray paw print, perhaps, or even a broken twig to lead her in the right direction. Every clue mattered now.

Olivia passed by the gardens and spotted Desmond in the middle of a tense conversation with one of the wedding vendors. She kept her distance, eyes focused on the interaction. She couldn't make out all the details, but Desmond seemed to point at an itemized invoice, his hand trembling as he asked questions. After a few moments, Jill appeared and pulled him aside, her expression confused as they spoke, though the tension between them was clear. Desmond thrust a credit card at the vendor before storming off.

Olivia tugged on Elmer's leash, silently urging him forward. She needed to know what was going on.

Desmond's hurried walk was abruptly interrupted by none other than Victor, and instinctively, Olivia ducked behind a nearby cottage, pulling Elmer with her. She peeked around the corner just in time to catch their exchange.

"Whoa, you okay, Des?" Victor's voice was full of concern as he stepped aside to let Desmond pass.

Desmond straightened, clearly startled by Victor's sudden appearance. "Yeah, I'm fine," he muttered, brushing past him.

Victor wasn't having it. "You sure? Trouble in wedding land?"

Desmond paused, glancing at his friend before shaking his head. "Yeah, you could say that. Jill... she wants everything perfect. She's running up this enormous bill, and expects me to pay for it without even blinking."

Victor chuckled, trying to ease the tension. "Well, you are one of the biggest names in law around here. You can handle it, right?"

Desmond's expression faltered, panic flashing briefly across his face. "Yeah, of course... It's just—" He trailed off, then waved dismissively. "Money's not the issue. I just want it to go toward something worthwhile, something my parents would've supported. But this wedding? It's all fluff. All these ridiculous expenses, and for what?"

Victor chuckled again, slapping Desmond on the back. "Think of it this way, buddy. You're investing in your new wife. That's something that'll last, I hope."

Desmond stiffened at the comment, and Olivia could see the strain in his shoulders. His reassurance didn't seem to help. He paused for a moment before switching the conversation to something else. "So about signing those papers..." he started.

Victor interrupted with a casual pat on the arm. "I'm still thinking about it. But I need more time to look into things. Don't worry, Des. Things will turn out fine. Now, if you'll excuse me, I need to grab a couple of things from my car." With that, Victor turned and headed up the hill toward the parking area.

Desmond watched his friend walk off, his shoulders slumping in defeat. As he turned to head toward the guest cottages, Monica appeared, striding quickly up behind him.

Olivia crouched down with Elmer, watching as Monica followed her brother into the cottage. Without bothering to knock, she pushed the door open and disappeared inside. Olivia exchanged a wary look with Elmer, her suspicion growing with each passing second.

As Monica entered, Olivia stepped back into the shadows, straining to catch any snippets of their conversation.

"What did Victor say?" Monica's voice was sharp, demanding.

Inside, Olivia could see Desmond pacing, his hands clenched tightly. "About what?" he asked, his tone tight.

Monica let out an exasperated sigh. "Don't act like you don't know."

Desmond paused, frustrated. "He's still looking into it, and that's all I have for now. I can't push him any harder."

Olivia heard Desmond's voice rise in frustration. "What am I supposed to do, Monica? This wedding—it's a mess. The costs keep climbing, and I know I can't cover it. You're not making it easier, either."

Monica's posture stiffened, her voice sharp. "You think this is my fault? You've been hiding behind your career, your reputation. This affects my future too, Desmond, not just yours." She shook her head in exasperation. "You don't get it."

Desmond, clearly at his breaking point, threw his hands up in exasperation. "I get it, Monica. I really do. This is beyond my control. You can't just force people into things." He paused for a moment, the weight of his frustration hanging in the air. "You just can't."

Unperturbed, Monica closed the distance between them, her voice cold and calculating. "It's not enough, Des. You help me close this deal, or I'll make sure the world knows what a fraud you are."

With that, she stormed out of the cottage, leaving Desmond standing in the tense silence. Olivia exhaled, her thoughts a whirlwind. The words "fraud" echoed in her mind, adding another layer of confusion to everything. Was it somehow connected to Chardonnay's disappearance?

The more pieces she gathered, the more tangled everything seemed. There were too many secrets, too many questions, and Olivia was more determined than ever to uncover them all.

CHAPTER 10

T he afternoon sun streamed through the tall
windows of Dogwood Cottage's main hall, casting
a warm, golden light that filled the room. Dust motes
floated in the beams, giving the space an almost ethereal
quality. In the center of the room, the long banquet table
stood empty, awaiting its transformation with extravagant
linens and delicate tableware for the rehearsal dinner. A
heady mix of roses, lilies, and nervous energy filled the
air. Guests and vendors scurried about, absorbed in their
last-minute tasks. Outside, strips of tape and clusters of
flower arrangements outlined the ceremony site on the
front lawn, all setting the stage for Jill's carefully curated
wedding.

Inside, Olivia stood by the tall windows, keeping a
watchful eye on Benny, Ayla, and Chester, who were all
expected to play minor roles in the ceremony—*expected*

being the key word. Olivia had also brought Tulip in her cage, and the parrot sat perched nearby, observing the events unfolding around her. Chester perched on the windowsill, his tail flicking with impatience. Every few seconds, he shot a disdainful glance over his shoulder at Olivia, clearly displeased with the leash.

"How Jill expects a cat on a leash to do anything is beyond me," Olivia mused. Chester wasn't offering any commentary. *Better that way*, she decided, not wanting to imagine the barrage of unfiltered cat thoughts that might come pouring out.

Benny had a different idea of what constituted "good behavior." The exuberant dachshund dashed back and forth, his tiny legs a blur, pulling desperately toward the caterer, who was busy arranging appetizers. Olivia tightened her grip on his leash, trying to reel him in.

"Benny, you're here to steal hearts, not hors d'oeuvres," Olivia muttered with a sigh, her exasperation softening into affection. It was a challenge keeping Benny in check—he tripped over his own excitement at the best of times. Though Olivia hadn't heard much from Benny's thoughts before, his current inner monologue was loud and clear, startling her with its frantic intensity: *Treat, treat, treat, treat, TREAT!* Elmer lay stretched out at Olivia's feet, watching the chaos.

Suddenly, Katherine, Tulip's owner, appeared beside Olivia, her excitement bubbling over. "I'm hoping Jill will let Tulip have a special part in the ceremony," she said, her voice filled with hopeful optimism. "So far, Jill has only agreed to let her entertain during the rehearsal dinner, but Tulip is so charming! I'm sure after dinner Jill will see how perfect she'd be. But I figured it wouldn't hurt to bring her up here now, just in case."

Katherine leaned in a little closer, her voice dropping to a conspiratorial whisper. She paused, as if weighing whether to share more, and then added, "And with Chardonnay missing, there might be a need for her to fill in."

Olivia wasn't sure if Katherine meant for the comment to sound regretful about Chardonnay's disappearance, but her tone didn't quite come across that way. Her words seemed oddly sharp, hinting Chardonnay's absence presented an opportunity, not a loss.

Olivia's gaze shifted to Katherine, her suspicion growing. As she did, she caught sight of a faint red patch on Katherine's arm, just visible beneath her sleeve. It looked like the early signs of poison ivy, the rash still fresh. Olivia's mind raced as she tried to connect the dots. She had only seen poison ivy near her cottage. While it wasn't impossible for it to be elsewhere on the grounds, the coincidence felt off. *Was it just an accident, or was there something more behind Katherine's rushed actions and cryptic words?*

Olivia managed a polite smile, unsure how to respond. "Well, Tulip definitely has a... presence."

Right on cue, Tulip squawked from her cage. "Pretty bird! Pretty bird!" she shrieked, her voice echoing across the hall. Heads turned, guests stifled laughter, and Olivia winced as she glanced at Jill, who was deep in discussion with Edward over the floral arrangements. Jill shot a wary look at Tulip just as the parrot launched into a surprisingly on-key rendition of How Much is That Doggie in the Window—naturally transforming it into How Much is That Birdie in the Window.

"Quite the performer," Olivia chuckled as she tried to disentangle Benny's leash from Ayla's. "If Jill lets her join in, at least she won't have to worry about being heard."

In his excitement, Benny barreled into the leg of the table holding Tulip's cage. Without skipping a beat, the bird squawked sharply, "Mongrel!" Both Katherine and Olivia exchanged wide-eyed glances, taken aback by Tulip's quick retort. Katherine's cheeks flushed pink as she tutted at the parrot. "Quit fussing, you spoiled thing." Tulip, unfazed by the reprimand, cocked her head attentively, as if waiting for her next command.

Jill, looking frazzled, pulled herself away from Edward and strode toward the front steps, her heels clicking against the hardwood floor, sounding like orders being issued. Without a glance back, she called out, "Alright, everyone, let's get this rehearsal over with!" Her tone was that of a general rallying her troops for battle, a mix of determination and exhaustion etched on her face. She'd spent hours searching for Chardonnay that morning;

consequently, she seemed far less enthusiastic about wedding preparations and considerably more disheveled.

Olivia inhaled, gathering her charges. "Come on, guys," she whispered to the pets. "Let's try not to make Jill's day any more disastrous."

Elmer let out a soft sigh. Olivia caught his thought as it wafted through her mind: *Here we go.*

The sun blazed down over the lawn, casting a golden glow over the grassy aisle. Olivia gathered the animals at the head of the aisle, ready to follow Jill's direction. First up was Ayla, carrying a dainty basket of flower petals with pride. Olivia had hidden a few of Ayla's favorite treats among the petals to keep her motivated. As soon as Ayla caught the scent, her nostrils flared, and she began snuffling at the basket. In her excitement, she zigzagged her way down the aisle, shaking the basket with each step as she searched for the hidden treats. But as she neared the end of the aisle, Ayla's attention shifted. She perked up, hearing her owner's call, and trotted the last few steps with a graceful urgency, eager to complete her part in the ceremony.

Ayla trotted with confidence toward her owner, Shara, who shot a smug glance toward Rachel, Benny's owner. Rachel stood at the end of the aisle, looking frazzled as she tried to keep her attention on Benny, who was spinning in excited circles. His boundless energy prevented a slow, elegant stroll. Rachel called to him, trying to regain control, but before she could react, Benny's energy exploded. With a burst of excitement, he bolted forward.

"Benny, slow down!" Olivia called after him, her voice rising with exasperation. The dachshund seemed to believe he was competing in a race rather than participating in a rehearsal, zigzagging as he strained toward every interesting scent he encountered.

He veered off course, making a beeline for the nearest appetizer table, his floral collar already askew from his earlier antics. In a burst of agility, he snatched a canapé from a tray, swallowing it with glee before Olivia could even react. "Benny, no!" she exclaimed, but it was too late—the mischievous dachshund had already claimed his prize.

Finally, it was Chester's turn to make his entrance. He was supposed to walk down the aisle with Seth, leading the men's side of the bridal party like a regal mascot. Olivia had handed Chester off to Seth, who attempted to walk down the aisle but stopped abruptly, his gentle tugs on the leash yielding no movement from the cat.

"Come on, Chester," Seth encouraged, kneeling down to coax Chester along. When that didn't work, he tried a gentle tug, which momentarily caught Chester's attention, resulting in a few cautious steps forward. Just as things seemed to progress, a loud crash from the catering area rang out, startling Chester and prompting him to cling desperately to the runner.

With a flustered flush creeping into his cheeks, Seth had to kneel down to detach Chester from the decorative fabric. Defeated, he scooped the cat into his arms and marched down the aisle, cradling him like an exasperated parent holding a small child.

Olivia glanced over her shoulder to where Jill stood. Her composure was unraveling by the second. Her eyes, misty with a mix of stress and sagging sentimentality, darted over the chaotic scene assembled before her.

"This," she said, her voice heavy with desperation, "is where Chardonnay and I should be walking gracefully down the aisle." She turned to Olivia, her composure wavering as she fought to hold back tears.

Feeling the weight of responsibility, Olivia offered Jill a weak smile. The situation was feeling unbearable—Chardonnay's disappearance hanging like a shadow over the ceremony. Olivia's heart ached for Jill, but her mind was racing with questions. *Could Jill go through with the wedding without Chardonnay?* She had been such an integral part of the wedding. The uncertainty gnawed at Olivia, but she tried to push it aside.

"We'll figure it out, I promise," Olivia said to Jill, trying to sound more confident than she felt. Olivia, feeling like she needed to do something, had an idea. "Do you want to try it with Elmer?" Olivia asked gently, holding the leash out to Jill.

Olivia, trying to keep her own anxiety in check, spoke, her voice calm but insistent. "Jill, I know it's not ideal, but maybe… maybe Elmer could stand in for Chardonnay for the rehearsal. He's well-behaved," she paused before adding, "Most of the time.

Jill froze, her eyes narrowing with disbelief. "Elmer?" she snapped, a touch of incredulity in her voice. "You want that dog to stand in for Chardonnay? Absolutely not. He's not the star of the wedding. Chardonnay is."

Olivia sighed, trying to keep her tone measured. "I get it, Jill. But Elmer's a good dog. He might not be Chardonnay, but he can at least take her place temporarily—for the rehearsal. It's better than having no dog at all, right? He could stand in at the wedding too if he…needed to.", Olivia said hesitantly, not wanting to bring up the idea of not finding Chardonnay.

Jill blinked at Elmer, her expression skeptical as she tried to imagine him leading the wedding procession. "But… Elmer is so… unrefined," she said, wrinkling her nose. "Not to mention… he's a dog. A dog dog.

Jill's lips pressed into a thin line, her fingers twitching. "This wedding is about perfection." Her voice wavered, but her stubbornness was clear.

Jill let out a shaky breath, her hand trembling as she ran it through her hair. Her voice cracked as she fought back tears. "Chardonnay…She's supposed to be the star of the wedding."

Jill hesitated, her body stiffening, but there was a flicker of consideration in her eyes. "Fine. He'll do, for now. And for the wedding only if Chardonnay is not back by the time the ceremony starts, but that it's going to happen." she said, her voice tinged with reluctant acceptance. "But if that is the case, Elmer better not make a mockery of the moment. He better stand there and look dignified."

Olivia nodded, relieved. "Of course. I'll make sure of it."

Jill gave a single nod, her gaze still unsettled but resigned to the reality of the situation.

Half-listening, Elmer looked up, tail giving a weak wag as if reassuring Jill. But then, as though to punctuate his presence, he let out a low, rumbling belch. The scent of kibble filling the air.

Jill grimaced, wrinkling her nose. "Great. Can you make sure he doesn't do that during the wedding?"

Olivia couldn't help but chuckle. "I promise, he'll be on his best behavior."

Jill sighed, clearly not convinced. Shoulders slumped with defeat, she nodded and signaled to the string quartet to begin the music. She took Elmer's leash, glancing down at him wistfully as if trying to picture him as Chardonnay. Olivia felt another pang of guilt—Elmer wasn't the dog Jill wanted for this task, but it was the best they could do. Jill's face was a mixture of frustration and resignation. Elmer looked up at Jill with as much enthusiasm as he could muster for the task at hand. Olivia knelt next to him, whispering as she gestured toward the start of the aisle. "Just a short stroll. You can do it."

Reluctantly, Jill took a few uncertain steps, and Elmer followed her, staying in step. "He's... doing okay," Jill said, her voice laced with anxiety. "At least he's moving in the right direction." The pair continued down the aisle without incident. When they reached the end, Jill dropped the leash as if it had burned her, standing there stunned, unable to believe she had just made the walk without Chardonnay.

Elmer, realizing he was free, spotted Ayla sitting off to the side, savoring a flower petal with unrepentant delight. Forgetting the rehearsal entirely, he trotted over and flopped down beside Ayla, his tail wagging. *This is more fun,* he said.

Jill's composure faltered as she reviewed how her carefully planned ceremony had unraveled. Suddenly, Edward appeared at the front of the aisle, testing different vase sizes for an arrangement destined for the altar. As he placed a tall crystal vase on a pillar, a dark cloud suddenly rolled over the rehearsal. A powerful gust of wind swept through, and a few raindrops fell. Edward lost his grip on the vase, and the wind instantly claimed it, tossing it across the lawn and shattering into pieces.

The entire wedding party stood in stunned silence, mouths agape, as they watched the vase's destruction unfold. Jill looked up toward the sky, her frustration boiling over. She hurled the small bouquet someone had handed her to the ground. "It's a sign!" she squeaked, her voice cracking. Tears she had valiantly held back burst free and cascaded down her cheeks as she made a frantic dash toward the main house.

"Well, I guess that's that," the officiant muttered, shrugging as he tucked his Bible under his arm and headed for the parking lot, retreating from the disarray.

CHAPTER 11

T he chaotic aftermath of the rehearsal hung in the air as Olivia watched Jill hurry off, her face flushed with frustration and the weight of the ceremony's faltering plans. *So much for a smooth run-through.* The entire scene only left Olivia more unsettled about what was to come.

The dark clouds vanished as swiftly as they appeared, revealing the sun once again. Olivia wasn't one to put much stock in omens, but she couldn't deny that the sudden shift in weather felt a bit strange.

She lingered for a moment, her mind racing. Chardonnay's absence, odd guest behavior, and palpable tension overshadowed the wedding. The wedding was meant to be a celebration, yet Olivia couldn't shake the feeling that everything was slowly unraveling.

In the garden closest to the front lawn, Cassandra, Olivia's mother, was preparing her tarot reading station, a calm presence amidst the chaos. Dressed in flowing robes adorned with colorful beads, she seemed like a whimsical figure from another time, drawing curious glances from passing guests. She had an uncanny ability to exude a sense of peace, a quality that Olivia found both comforting and, at times, unsettling. There was an air of mystery to her mother Olivia had never fully understood—and today, with the strange atmosphere of the wedding, it was even more pronounced.

Jill intended Cassandra's tarot card readings to serve as entertainment during the rehearsal dinner and after-party, but Olivia wondered if the readings would become more than just a fun distraction. She wondered if they had picked up on the same unsettling energy she had felt all day. *What had the cards shown today? Were they just a source of amusement, or did they hold a deeper truth about the tension swirling around Jill, Monica, and the other guests?*

Olivia knew well that her mother never sugar-coated her readings. Cassandra would lay out the cards as they appeared, no matter how harsh the truths they showed. If the cards pointed to trouble or hidden secrets, Cassandra would not soften the blow. Olivia had seen it before—people sitting at her mother's table, eager for insight, only to be confronted with truths they weren't prepared to hear.

As Cassandra arranged the cards on the table, Olivia's gaze lingered on her mother, a slight frown creasing her forehead. There was something about the way Cassandra was moving—slow and deliberate, as though preparing for more than just a casual reading. Olivia could almost feel the quiet pulse of expectation in the air, and for the first time, she wondered if it was more than just wedding nerves. *Was her mother sensing something too?*

Olivia wove her way through the aftermath of the chaotic rehearsal, Benny, Ayla, and Elmer trotting beside her. Their owners had relinquished them as soon as the trial run was over, and Olivia had resumed her responsibility of keeping them in line. As she sank into the chair across from her mother, she ignored Ayla's eager attempts to snatch a passing treat, offering her mother a weary smile. "Hey, Mom," Olivia greeted, her voice tinged with exhaustion. "Please tell me you've seen something in the cards that could help me find Chardonnay."

Cassandra shuffled her tarot deck with unusual seriousness, her focus fixed on the cards in her hands. "Earlier, while preparing for the event, I did a reading. It was... unsettling," she intoned, her voice carrying a weight that made Olivia sit up straighter. "Unsettling how?" Olivia asked, a sense of dread beginning to pool in her stomach. Cassandra flipped over the Tower card, its ominous imagery sending a chill down Olivia's spine. "There's a dark energy surrounding this event," she explained. "Danger and deceit lurk in the shadows, tied to both the bride and the groom. But it's unclear whether the threat is coming from within or outside the wedding."

Olivia's heart raced, and she leaned forward, hanging on her mother's every word. Cassandra's tone grew more somber as she continued. "There's more happening here than you realize. You need to be cautious, Olivia." She paused, taking a deep breath before adding, "But I haven't seen anything specific regarding Chardonnay."

The air between them grew heavy, and Olivia's chest tightened. Her mother's readings were always cryptic but rarely wrong. *A dark energy?* The wedding's escalating tension, coupled with Chardonnay's disappearance, made the prediction seem perfectly fitting.

"Of course," Olivia murmured, running a hand through her hair in frustration. "Just what we need—dark energy. I've got barking dogs, a squawking parrot, and a missing poodle. Can't we just have one smooth event?" Cassandra's lips twitched with a knowing smile. "Just don't get caught up in something you can't handle, Liv. This wedding is oozing with unsettling vibes." "Thanks, Mom," Olivia replied, her voice light, but her heart weighed down with worry. "I'll do my best to avoid a catastrophe." She gestured toward Benny and Ayla, who had twisted themselves around her feet while Elmer observed, looking thoroughly amused by the antics. "Right now, though, I need to get these guys back to the cottage. I'll be back later for the rehearsal dinner." Olivia stood, haunted by her mother's warning.

As Olivia scanned the crowd, looking for Seth to retrieve Chester, she noticed Monica near the makeshift altar, deep in conversation with Victor. The tension between them was obvious. Monica leaned in closer, her body language intense, while Victor remained stiff, his posture guarded, like a man trapped in a conversation he didn't want to have.

Suddenly, Tulip, ever the drama queen, let out a piercing squawk, shattering the tension. "Help! Help!" she cried. Laughter rippled through the guests gathered for afternoon appetizers, but Katherine, visibly embarrassed, rushed to hush her. "No, Tulip, hello, not help," she scolded, her cheeks turning pink. Tulip paused, cocking her head as if considering the reprimand before launching into another round of squawks. Olivia couldn't help but shake her head, a grin tugging at her lips. "Looks like we all need help, Tulip," she muttered under her breath.

Turning to Katherine, she asked, "Want me to take Tulip back to the cottage along with these two? She gestured toward Benny and Ayla, still distracted by the catering tables' smells. "Yes! That would be perfect," Katherine replied, her gratitude clear as she headed toward the bar, leaving Olivia to juggle the pets. Olivia spotted Seth nearby and moved to retrieve Chester, who was handed over with little fuss.

With Tulip's cage hoisted on her hip, Chester tucked under her arm, leashes in hand, and Elmer trotting behind, Olivia made her way through the crowd. "At least the walk back is downhill," she thought to herself, nudging Elmer along with her foot. He, unlike the others, seemed to be the only one keeping himself together. Tulip's cries continued unabated. "Help! Help!"

"I hear you," Olivia whispered, rolling her eyes with a soft chuckle. "At this point, I think we all need it." As the squawks continued, Olivia's attention drifted back to Monica, who was now standing near an appetizer table, having finished her conversation with Victor. She stiffened at the sound of Tulip's cries, and Olivia couldn't help but notice the brief flicker of discomfort that crossed Monica's face. Her lips pressed into a thin line, and her eyes narrowed for a moment, as if Tulip's persistent squawking was unsettling her.

Olivia paused mid-step, unsure if she'd imagined the reaction. Monica turned away, pretending to fiddle with her phone, but her tense posture didn't escape Olivia's notice. Something about Monica's response didn't sit right. Shaking off the feeling, Olivia continued on her way, trying to ignore the odd discomfort that had settled in her stomach.

As she rounded the corner of the main house, Olivia spotted Thomas, the journalist Monica had mentioned to Desmond, standing alone, scribbling furiously in his notebook. Olivia had seen him over the last couple of days, staying to the fringes of the events, always observing, always taking notes. Cassandra's earlier warning about danger and deceit echoed in her mind, and she studied Thomas, her suspicions flaring. He was so absorbed in his notes, completely unaware of the world around him.

Why was he really here? What was he reporting on?
More questions, Olivia thought, questions she couldn't yet answer.

With her arms full, her heart racing, and Tulip's persistent squawking filling the air, Olivia realized one thing for certain: time was slipping away. The storm Cassandra had foreseen was gathering on the horizon, and it was coming faster than Olivia had expected.

Olivia nudged open the pet cottage door with her hip, balancing two leashes, a parrot cage, and Chester the cat—all while avoiding tripping over her own feet. The door creaked as it swung open, and she let out a quiet sigh of relief. *I haven't lost anyone in transit,* she thought, glancing down at Elmer, who trotted at her side with his tail wagging. Once inside, Chester sprang from Olivia's arms with remarkable agility, landing on the plush armchair in the corner like a practiced acrobat. He settled into his usual spot, as if nothing had changed. Olivia couldn't help but smile. *Finally* came Chester's faint thought, his tone thick with irritation and a hint of anxiety.

Elmer, meanwhile, flopped onto Olivia's bed like he'd just run a marathon, burying his face in the pillows. His sigh of contentment spoke volumes—clearly, being on his best behavior had taken its toll. Olivia unhooked Benny and Ayla from their leashes. Ayla sauntered over to the plush dog bed near the window, her gaze locked on Olivia, radiating that regal air she often assumed. *Well?* Ayla's thought cut through, sharp and demanding, as if awaiting Olivia's immediate attention. *Is my throne prepared?* With a playful roll of her eyes, Olivia dutifully fluffed the dog bed. "There you go, Your Majesty." Ayla sniffed approvingly, easing herself into the bed and holding her head high in regal satisfaction. Olivia glanced around, spotting Ayla's bag of beauty accouterments, she rifled through it, finding the misting spray and the paw balm. She had been keeping up with Ayla's routine as well as she could, but she had to admit she hadn't stayed perfectly on schedule. *Something is better than nothing, right?,* Olivia thought to herself as she spritzed the dog with spray and rubbed her down, then carefully wiped each paw with a nearby towel and applied a small amount of balm, working into the pads of her paws. *This dog has softer hands than I do,* thought Olivia.

Meanwhile, Benny—a ball of uncontainable energy—began tearing through the room, his tiny paws a blur as he raced in wild circles. He clawed at Chester's chair, earning a sharp, disapproving glare from the cat, who was unamused by his antics. Tulip, who had been chattering and squawking nonstop during the walk back, had quieted surprisingly once they entered the cottage. Olivia had set her cage on the counter, stretching her sore arms, while Tulip shifted on her perch. Just as Benny zipped past, he barked up at the cage, causing Tulip to squawk back without hesitation. "Shut up, you mongrel!" she squawked, her voice sharp and echoing through the cottage. Benny paused, tilting his head, confused, before resuming his energetic laps around the room. *This is the second time she's thrown that out there today,* Olivia thought, raising an eyebrow at the parrot's choice of words.

"Help! Help! Woof! Woof!" Tulip cried, her voice urgent and oddly well-timed. The room fell silent for a moment, and Olivia raised an eyebrow, intrigued. "Help... woof?" Olivia repeated, a spark of curiosity igniting in her chest. *Could Tulip know something about Chardonnay's disappearance?* Her mind flashed back to Monica's odd reaction to the parrot's earlier cries for help, but now something else was nagging at her.

Olivia stepped closer to the cage, peering intently at the vibrant bird. "Tulip, did you see what happened to Chardonnay?" she asked, her voice serious now, holding her breath in anticipation. It wasn't a stretch to think the parrot might have seen something. Whomever took Chardonnay would have had to walk past her to get to Chardonnay. She had a cloth draped over her cage, but it was thin; she might have seen shadows or heard something.

To her surprise, Tulip bobbed her head in an exaggerated nod. "Help! Help! Woof! Woof!" she responded, this time with a hint of excitement. Olivia's heart raced. *Was Tulip mimicking the sounds she'd heard the night Chardonnay disappeared? Or was this just another bizarre parrot quirk?* "Did someone take Chardonnay?" Olivia pressed, her hope rising. Tulip's response was immediate, but this time, Olivia froze. The phrase was too specific, too familiar: "Quit fussing, you spoiled thing." It was Katherine's voice. She'd said that exact phrase earlier to Tulip, when the parrot had been squawking at the wedding preparations. Olivia's stomach tightened, the unease settling in. *Had Tulip overheard something more—something from Katherine?*

"What else can you tell me?" Olivia asked, her frustration mounting. The bird gave a satisfied tilt of her head before squawking loudly, "Pretty bird! Pretty bird! Tulip! Pretty bird!" Olivia sighed, exasperated. The bird's cryptic words only deepened her suspicions. *Was there more to Katherine's jealousy over Chardonnay than met the eye? Could she have taken the dog, hoping to give Tulip the chance to steal the spotlight? Was the bird's mimicry a clue, or just a strange coincidence?* But then the "Shut up, mongrel!" didn't add up. Katherine had been doting on all the animals throughout the weekend. It didn't fit with the kindness she'd shown. Olivia frowned, the pieces not quite aligning. She couldn't shake the unsettling feeling that Tulip's words weren't random. Something darker was at play, and whether or not Tulip knew it, she was a key witness.

Poking her head into the bedroom, Olivia called out, "You coming with me, big guy? I think it's time to head back to the main house and do some more investigating." Elmer let out a long, disgruntled sigh—his version of Are you kidding me? With a dramatic roll, he turned his back to her, offering a comical display of protest. "Fair enough," Olivia chuckled. "Guess I'm on my own for this one." She gave the chaotic yet strangely comforting cottage one last glance before stepping outside into the warm afternoon air, the intoxicating scent of blooming flowers filling her senses.

CHAPTER 12

As Olivia made her way back toward the main house, Tulip's persistent squawks echoed in her mind: "Help! Help! Woof! Woof!" But it wasn't just the bird's cries that unsettled her—it was the way Tulip had repeated phrases that seemed eerily familiar, phrases that sounded as if they came straight from Katherine. Olivia's mind raced, wondering how these odd repetitions fit into the puzzle. *Could they be a clue, or just a strange coincidence?*

As the afternoon stretched on, Dogwood Cottage's lawn buzzed with the sound of laughter, the clink of glasses, and the gentle strains of a string quartet drifting through the warm air. The soft golden light of the setting sun bathed the guests, who milled about, flitting between the outdoor bar and the clusters of seating. Polite conversation and occasional bursts of laughter filled the air as guests sipped cocktails and exchanged pleasantries.

Olivia couldn't help but marvel at the elaborate pre-party, wondering if this was just the way of things with such a large gathering. *I guess with this many* guests, *you have to entertain them somehow,* she thought, her gaze sweeping over the crowd. The pre-parties felt like complete events on their own, with the wedding appearing as a small part of the grand spectacle of elaborate gatherings and ongoing preparations.

Olivia scanned the crowd, her gaze sharp and purposeful. Chardonnay's absence weighed on her, a constant presence that gnawed at her thoughts, making everything else feel a little off-kilter. Along with that, other nagging feelings were settling in, each one adding to the unease she couldn't shake. The mingling after the rehearsal felt like an opportunity—one she needed to navigate carefully. The tension in the air was palpable, and as much as Olivia wanted to press for answers, she knew she had to be subtle.

When her eyes landed on Rachel near the bar, Olivia's pulse quickened. Rachel was doing her best to seem at ease, but Olivia could see the strain around her smile, the tension in her posture betraying her calm facade, hinting at an unease she was trying to hide. Her usual elegance seemed worn thin, and her laughter, though polite, was sharp and brittle as she chatted with another guest.

"Hey, Rachel," Olivia greeted, trying to keep her voice light. "Surviving Benny's antics today, I see?"

Rachel rolled her eyes dramatically, a faint smile tugging at her lips. "Barely. I love the little rascal, but I swear he has a gift for public embarrassment." The smile faded quickly, and the humor not reaching her eyes, and Olivia caught a flicker of something else—anxiety, perhaps? The momentary tension slipped away.

"Any news on Chardonnay?" she asked, her voice a little too casual. "Not yet," Olivia replied, trying to meet her casual tone. "I'm piecing things together. Do you remember anything odd happening last night?"

Rachel's fingers tightened around her drink, her eyes darting away for just a moment, as though weighing whether to answer. She finally spoke, her voice faltering. "Well, I thought I heard rustling outside my window," she admitted, her words coming slowly. "But I didn't check it out—I figured it was just a raccoon or something." She forced a nervous laugh, trying to mask her discomfort. Olivia raised an eyebrow. "A raccoon? I haven't seen any around here, but I suppose it's possible." Rachel let out a nervous laugh. "Right? I didn't want to go check and end up face-to-face with a raccoon, especially not with everything going on before the wedding."

Olivia's mind raced, a thousand questions forming, but she held her composure. "I just didn't want to sound paranoid," Rachel said, her voice taking on an edge of frustration mixed with embarrassment. "I'm used to city noises—sirens, car alarms—not wildlife rustling around." Her gaze flicked away, avoiding Olivia's. Olivia nodded thoughtfully, her voice softening. "Understandable. But if you think of anything else, it could be really helpful." Rachel's tense posture loosened a fraction, but her eyes betrayed a flicker of something else—guilt? Fear? She lowered her voice, just loud enough for Olivia to hear. "I will. I hope you find Chardonnay soon. Jill's been... well, let's just say she's not exactly sitting in wedding bliss with her missing."

Managing a small smile, Olivia excused herself, weaving through the crowd as she tried to gather her thoughts. Her mind churned with everything she had learned so far—the clues, the cryptic conversations, the strange behavior of certain guests. Each interaction seemed to add another layer to the mystery, but nothing was fitting together yet. *What was the connection between the missing dog and the strange tension in the air? Why had Chardonnay disappeared so suddenly? Why did everyone appear so... on edge?*

Olivia watched as Rachel turned to rejoin the other guests, her body language still tight. There was something about the conversation that didn't sit right with Olivia. The way Rachel had brushed off the idea of hearing rustling outside, the way her eyes had flicked away when Olivia mentioned it—it all felt too rehearsed. *Was she hiding something?* The mention of Chardonnay's absence, though casual, seemed forced, like she was trying too hard to sound sympathetic. Jill's absence of wedding bliss was clearly more than just an offhand comment. *Was*

Rachel subtly distancing herself from the situation, or had she been more involved than she let on? Olivia's thoughts swirled as she considered Rachel's reaction. Guilt, fear... or maybe both? There had been something guarded in her tone when she said, "I hope you find Chardonnay soon." *Was that genuine concern, or was she trying to hide something?* Her mind raced through the implications. *If Rachel had noticed anything—if she had heard anything last night—why hadn't she shared more? Was she protecting someone? Or was she simply afraid of being involved?* There was a nagging feeling in Olivia's gut that Rachel knew more than she was letting on. She couldn't shake the suspicion that Rachel held a piece of the puzzle, but which piece, exactly? And how did it fit with everything else that had been happening? Olivia cast one last look in Rachel's direction, still deep in conversation with a guest, her posture once again closed off. The mystery deepened, and with it, Olivia's need to uncover the truth. But for now, all she could do was wait—and watch.

As she moved through the crowd, she overheard bits and pieces of conversations, but they all seemed trivial—nothing to help with the puzzle she was trying to solve. The laughter, the clinking of glasses, and the soft strains of the string quartet only heightened the sense of dissonance in Olivia's mind. Everything felt off, but she couldn't quite put her finger on why. Eventually, she found herself near a small cluster of guests where Desmond was deep in conversation with Raymond, the caterer. Olivia's eyes narrowed as she tried to pick up any useful details. Desmond was speaking in low tones, and though she strained to overhear, the constant flow of people and chatter made it difficult to catch anything concrete. Just as Olivia was about to give up on eavesdropping, Desmond glanced over and met her gaze. He gave her a brief, strained smile that didn't quite reach his eyes. There was something there—something unsettled about him. As though he were carrying the weight of a thousand unspoken concerns.

Her gaze drifted to the back of the garden where Monica stood. She was watching Victor intently as he spoke with a couple of other men, her posture rigid, her expression unreadable. Olivia's instincts flared—something about Monica's focus on Victor felt more than just casual interest. She couldn't explain it, but it nagged at her. There was a connection here that hadn't yet shown itself. Olivia's curiosity overruled her hesitation, and with a quick glance back at Desmond and Raymond, she followed Monica from a distance. Her heart raced as she maneuvered through the guests. The possibilities swirled in her mind—*what was Monica hiding? What had she missed?* Olivia couldn't shake the feeling that Monica might be the key to the lead she'd been waiting for.

As Olivia trailed behind, Monica's face remained a mask of calm, but Olivia couldn't forget the tension she'd sensed in their earlier encounters. When Monica paused at the bar to refresh her drink, Olivia saw her opening.

"Monica," Olivia called. "Got a minute?" Monica turned, her smile fading into something more guarded.

"Olivia. What's up?"

"I was just wondering if you've noticed anything... unusual today. Anything off with the guests, or the wedding plans?" Olivia asked, her eyes narrowing. Monica's gaze flickered over Olivia's shoulder, her brow furrowing. "It's been chaotic. Lots of people to manage, not enough time," she replied, her tone defensive. "Mm-hmm," Olivia responded, maintaining her casual demeanor. "Just checking in. With Chardonnay still missing, I wanted to make sure nothing else is slipping through the cracks."

"Everything's under control," Monica said, forcing a smile. "We've been working hard to keep things on track. You know how it is—keep the drama low until the big day." The tension in the air was thick, but Olivia didn't miss the way Monica's cheerful tone didn't quite match her body language. Monica's focus shifted, and for a moment she seemed lost in thought. She sighed, her eyes drifting toward the horizon, her voice dropping to a murmur. "I just... I really wish Mom and Dad were here to see this." The unexpected sadness in her voice caught Olivia off guard. It wasn't the typical coldness Monica usually projected. There was a brief pause, and Monica blinked, as if snapping herself back to the present. Her expression quickly hardened, and she cleared her throat, dismissing the moment as if it had never happened.

Returning her focus to Olivia, she said, "Anyway, I'm sure you've got things to deal with," Monica added, waving her hand dismissively.

Olivia watched Monica as she turned and made her way back into the cottage, her steps purposeful but quick. Olivia paused for a moment, gathering her thoughts before following her inside. But the odd remark about their parents hung in her mind. It felt out of place—why mention them now, of all times? With everything that had happened, it seemed like an unusual thing to bring up. She pushed it to the back of her mind for now. *Weddings do strange things to people*, she reminded herself. As Olivia stepped inside, the air buzzed with laughter and conversation. But her focus immediately sharpened. Scanning the room, her eyes locked onto Thomas, furiously scribbling in his notebook at a table tucked in the corner. *Where do you fit into all of this, Thomas?* The question lingered, unanswered, as she tried to make sense of everything.

Olivia felt the pressure mounting as the tangled web around her seemed to tighten. She needed to find real clues—something concrete. Leaving the social chaos behind, she resolved to spend the remaining time before the evening's rehearsal dinner searching for Chardonnay and uncovering whatever else was at play.

Olivia wandered along the gravel path at the edge of the property, the crunch of her shoes the only sound breaking the stillness. The late afternoon sun hung low, casting long shadows over the expansive grounds of Dogwood Cottage. Above her, the towering dogwood trees swayed in the breeze, their pink and white blossoms shimmering in the fading light. She had spoken to several guests, but no one had seen anything unusual—no one had noticed anything suspicious or had any other information about Chardonnay's disappearance.

She headed toward the small wooded area behind the larger guest cottages, her eyes scanning the ground as she moved. The area was eerily quiet, save for the occasional rustle of leaves and the distant chirp of a bird. Olivia's sharp gaze flicked over the earth, looking for any sign—footprints, scraps of fabric, or anything that might seem out of place. Near the edge of the forest, she crouched, her heart skipping a beat as she noticed a set of faint paw prints in the dirt leading off into the trees. Nearby, she noticed a broken branch, twisted and bent as though something—or someone—had been dragged through. Her breath caught. *Had whoever took Chardonnay dragged her into the woods? Had they left her there, or worse?*

Determined, Olivia followed the trail, her focus unyielding as she stepped carefully, keeping her eyes trained on the ground. As she went further, she became more certain that someone had hidden something here—something that could show what really happened to Chardonnay. Yet, as she searched, the clues remained elusive, and her frustration grew.

By the time she reached the edge of the property again, the sky had shifted, the warm orange glow of sunset casting a gentle hue over everything. Realizing how much time had passed, Olivia knew it was time to return to her cottage. She had to make sure everything was ready for the upcoming rehearsal dinner. As she walked back, a nagging feeling lingered, as though she was still missing something. Reaching the front door, she glanced over her shoulder, half-expecting to spot a clue she had overlooked. But the property remained calm—too calm. With a quiet sigh, she stepped inside, the sense of urgency she had felt while searching replaced by the looming pressure of the evening ahead. Too many questions remained unanswered.

CHapTer 13

That evening, the air at Dogwood Cottage hummed with an electric sense of anticipation as the rehearsal dinner unfolded. Softly glowing lanterns lined the garden, their warm light flickering and casting shadows across the manicured lawn. Guests wandered through the space, their laughter blending with the gentle hum of music in the background. The fragrant scent of freshly cut flowers, arranged by Edward with great care, wafted through the evening air. Olivia paused for a moment, inhaling deeply, hoping the tranquil setting might help calm her frayed nerves.

Olivia stood on the porch with Elmer by her side, watching the vibrant activity around her. A lively hum filled the air, a symphony of laughter, chatter, and clinking glasses. Yet, beneath it all, a heavy weight pressed on her heart. Chardonnay's absence overshadowed the joyous occasion. The rehearsal dinner—the last big event before the wedding—should have been celebratory, but Olivia couldn't shake a feeling that something darker loomed beneath the surface.

From where she stood, Olivia could see Raymond and his team of wait staff bustling back and forth between the kitchen and the assortment of tables nestled under the soft glow of string lights. A bar with an enticing spread of hors d'oeuvres beckoned guests to indulge their appetites while the main dinner would soon unfold inside the cottage.

Just then, Jill swept into the space like a storm, her every step deliberate but betraying the chaos within. She wore a sleek cocktail gown, looking like a bride trying to hold it all together amidst the whirlwind of wedding preparations. Her smile was bright, but it didn't quite reach her eyes. "Isn't this just perfect?" she said, her voice rising with a forced excitement that felt out of place. There was an undercurrent of tension in her tone, a disconnect between the words and the worry that was plain on her face.

Her gaze swept over the gathering, but her eyes quickly found Olivia's, the smile faltering for just a moment. "Everything is perfect! Except... except..."

Olivia's heart clenched, knowing what was coming. The 'except' hung in the air like a heavy sigh, the unspoken truth clear. Jill's brave façade cracked, her shoulders slumping as the reality of Chardonnay's absence took hold of her. She tried to pull herself together, but the cracks were widening. Without another word, Jill turned and hurried toward her suite upstairs, the carefully composed image of the bride slipping away with each step. The raw emotion behind her rushed forward, retreating just as quickly as she disappeared from view.

Shara and Rachel exchanged a glance, concern written across their faces. They excused themselves from their conversations, following Jill upstairs with quiet urgency, their expressions clouded with worry for their friend. Olivia stood there for a moment, watching the scene, a gnawing sense of helplessness twisting inside her. The wedding may have moved forward around them, but for Jill, a vital piece was missing—and it was impossible for her to ignore.

Olivia and Elmer entered the main area for the rehearsal dinner, scanning the crowded room. Her eyes flashed over the lively guests as she searched for Katherine and Monica. Neither seemed to have noticed the commotion. Monica was across the room, effortlessly charming a small group of women, her smile confident and at ease. Nearby, Katherine fussed over Tulip, who stood on a rhinestone-studded perch near the window, preparing for her performance later in the evening. The bird's loud squawks pierced the air, creating a comical contrast to the otherwise refined atmosphere.

As Olivia's gaze lingered on Monica, something caught her attention—a bright red patch on the back of Monica's leg, just visible beneath her dress. The patch stood out starkly against her otherwise flawless skin. Olivia squinted, a sense of recognition tugging at her. The mark resembled the rash she'd once gotten from poison ivy, its shape and intensity eerily familiar.

Curiosity piqued, Olivia moved closer, Elmer trotting by her side. She squinted, trying to get a better look at the mark on Monica's leg. Her mind raced, trying to recall where she had seen something similar. *Who had it been?* Just as the thought lingered, Elmer's voice broke through her concentration, his tone calm and direct.

Itchy, he said, his words as matter-of-fact as ever as he observed the two women.

Olivia's pulse quickened as the pieces clicked into place. The other red patch—she'd seen it on Katherine's arm. Glancing back at Katherine, Olivia watched her absentmindedly scratch at her arm, the movement almost subconscious. Her gaze then flicked back to Monica, who was now shifting uncomfortably, as though trying to ease an itch.

The sight of the rash on both women sent a jolt through Olivia. Alarm bells rang in her mind. She wasn't sure if there was poison ivy anywhere else on the property, but she knew for certain one place it existed: outside the back of her cottage.

Olivia's heart skipped a beat at the connection. She glanced from Monica to Katherine, both of whom had seemed unaffected by their surroundings and the drama unfolding with Jill. *Did Chardonnay's disappearance somehow involve those two?* The itchy patches on their skin, the strange tension with the other guests... everything felt a little too suspicious to be a coincidence.

Just then, Edward Barnes rushed past, struggling to balance a bouquet of exotic orchids in one hand and an enormous arrangement of delicate dogwood blossoms in the other. "Why anyone needs ten varieties of flowers to 'symbolize purity' is beyond me," he muttered under his breath, a mix of frustration and disbelief evident on his face.

"Need help?" Olivia called out.

Edward paused, shooting her a grateful look that quickly turned exasperated. "Only if you have the magical ability to prevent these plants from wilting under ridiculous expectations," he replied, adjusting his grip before disappearing through the garden entrance. Olivia pondered the bizarre necessity of yet more floral arrangements for a wedding held on a property that was blooming with natural beauty.

The rehearsal dinner had transformed the main area of Dogwood Cottage into a picturesque scene worthy of a glossy bridal magazine. A long, polished wooden table stretched the length of the room, its surface dressed with a delicate lace runner that wound its way between vases bursting with vibrant floral displays. Orchids, lilies, and signature dogwood blossoms created an enchanting tapestry of deep purples, soft pinks, and crisp whites that glowed in the warm, golden light. Candles flickered in elegant glass holders scattered along the table, casting dancing shadows over elaborate china and sparkling silverware. Each place settings was meticulously arranged, with dark green napkins folded into precise triangles gracing ceramic plates, each crowned by a gold-edged card bearing a name written in graceful cursive.

The soft crackle of the stone fireplace added to the ambiance, making the room feel snug despite its grandeur; it was perhaps more for atmosphere than necessity, given the warmth of the summer evening. String lights crisscrossed the beamed ceiling overhead, twinkling like constellations captured indoors. The glow from the fire illuminated the long windows, offering glimpses of the moonlit garden beyond, where the shadows of trees danced in the gentle evening breeze.

Olivia positioned herself at the edge of the room, blending in to observe the unfolding rehearsal dinner without drawing attention. As her gaze scanned the space, she spotted Desmond in a tense conversation with Raymond, the caterer, who was holding a pristine silver serving bowl. Olivia couldn't make out their words, but when Desmond cut off the discussion and strode away, she saw Raymond roll his eyes before heading to the kitchen. He placed the bowl on the counter with a frustrated thud, his voice floating over to Olivia. "Throw this out, I guess. Since the dog isn't here, we don't need it. Rich people. Humans would fight over the steak cuts in this bowl, much less feed it to their dog."

As Raymond retreated to the other side of the kitchen, his footsteps echoed. He muttered, "Leaving that dog at home would have saved everyone—myself included—a lot of trouble."

Olivia had known Raymond for years, and while he'd always had a soft spot for animals—dogs in particular—there was something unsettling about the way he handled the situation. His irritation was tangible, his movements sharp as he placed the bowl on the counter. The frustration in his voice as he spoke to no one sent a ripple of doubt through Olivia. She questioned whether his anger stemmed from pressure or something more. *Did his growing weariness with the pet duties have anything to do with Chardonnay's disappearance?* She couldn't help but wonder if Raymond might be more involved in the mystery than she first thought.

Raymond returned to the kitchen doorway, waving Olivia over. Curiosity piqued, she approached Elmer on her heels and he held out the same serving bowl she had seen him take in. "Somebody may as well enjoy this. What do you say, Elmer?" he quipped, then glanced at Olivia. "Do you mind?"

She glanced down at Elmer, who was giving her a pleading look, his eyes wide with that unmistakable "pleeeease"—like a child begging for a toy in the store. "Totally fine," she chuckled, more than happy to oblige.

Raymond placed the bowl on the floor around the corner in the kitchen, giving Elmer privacy from the curious eyes of the guests. The dog paused, then dove into the food, his focus narrowing to the meal before him as he devoured it without hesitation.

As Elmer enjoyed his feast, Olivia turned her attention back to the room, where the buzz of conversation and laughter seemed to hum beneath a thin layer of tension. At the far end of the long table, Jill stood, glass in hand, preparing to make her toast. Her voice, strong and clear, filled the room. "Everyone!" she called, commanding attention. "I want to propose a toast to all of you—our guests, who've traveled far and wide to make this day special."

For a moment, her smile faltered, and there was a flicker of something darker in her eyes, something that didn't quite match the cheer in her tone. She took a deep breath, steadying herself. "Even though the star of the show isn't here at the moment," she said, her voice thick with emotion, "I have faith that she will return before the ceremony."

Then, almost imperceptibly, her expression shifted. Her eyes narrowed, and she raised her glass higher, her voice now sharp. "But if anyone here knows anything about what happened to Chardonnay, I will find out. And I promise, I won't be kind when I do." The room went still, and for a brief moment, the air felt suffocating. Her gaze swept across the guests, lingering just a little too long on a few faces.

A quick, tight smile erased Jill's momentary vulnerability as she straightened. "But," she continued, shifting back into her cheerful tone, "let's focus on the joy of today. To good friends, good times, and the perfect wedding!" The glass lifted, and the guests hesitantly followed her lead, clinking their glasses together.

As the guests drifted back into their conversations, the clinking of silverware and quiet murmurs filling the air, the evening's entertainment began—Tulip's performance. The parrot perched gracefully on her rhinestone-studded perch, a gleaming figure under the soft lights. With a confident squawk, she launched into a surprisingly on-key rendition of a popular love song, her voice cutting through the murmur of the crowd, drawing a few amused glances and appreciative chuckles.

Tulip's melodies transitioned effortlessly, shifting from the lyrics of the song into a captivating instrumental tune. Playful yet calming, the music's odd mix captivated the crowd. Katherine stood proudly nearby, her beaming smile impossible to miss as she watched her prized bird perform. She occasionally cast a subtle, smug look toward Jill, as if silently claiming the spotlight for Tulip—something Jill either overlooked or pretended not to see.

Overwhelmed by the day's swirling emotions, Jill, seated at the far end of the table, failed to pay attention to the party going on around her. Her gaze drifted; she seemed oblivious to both the performance and the enthusiastic applause. She had retreated into herself, consumed by the hole that Chardonnay's absence had left in the celebration.

CHAPTER 14

As the evening wore on, Olivia's senses heightened as she moved through the crowd, noting every detail—every subtle shift in energy. Her gaze lingered on Monica, who seemed to glide from one conversation to the next, her words polished, her expressions charming, but there was something cold in her eyes. Monica exchanged tight, practiced smiles with the guests, but it was the fleeting moments when her gaze met Victor's that Olivia couldn't ignore. There was something there—something unspoken. Their interactions were sharp, filled with a tension that crackled just beneath the surface. Monica would lean in, her words quiet and measured, while Victor remained stiff, his posture rigid as if caught in an invisible tug-of-war. Their conversations seemed private, veiled in layers of formality, but Olivia could sense the undercurrent of strain that hung between them.

Olivia's attention returned to Desmond. She had spotted him a few times throughout the evening, but now, standing at the far end of the room, he looked like a man undone. He was no longer the polished groom-to-be, charming and confident, but a man unraveling, his shoulders tense and stiff, his expression taut with frustration. Desmond's eyes flickered as he scanned the room, his posture so rigid it was almost painful to watch. He was standing near the bar, exchanging a few words with a group of guests, but his words seemed distracted, disconnected, as if his mind was miles away.

The tension between Monica and Desmond seemed to have intensified. Desmond's usual composure had faded, replaced by the strained demeanor of a man clearly overwhelmed—by the wedding, his family, and something else Olivia couldn't quite place.

When Desmond turned and met Monica's gaze, the exchange felt loaded. More than just a fleeting glance. Olivia caught it—a subtle but unmistakable flicker between them. Desmond's mouth tightened, his jaw clenching as though he were trying to contain something, while Monica's smile curled tight, almost predatory. Olivia couldn't shake the feeling that whatever was playing out between them had a connection to the larger mystery she was desperately trying to piece together.

Just then, Olivia's gaze landed on Thomas, the investigative journalist, sitting near the back. Scribbling notes into his small leather notebook, his focus shifted between Monica, Desmond, and Jill, his brow furrowing with concern. He didn't seem to care about the toasts or the festivities unfolding around him. *He's definitely not here just for wedding coverage,* Olivia thought.

"Olivia, have you found out anything about Chardonnay?" Jill's voice cut through Olivia's thoughts, her gaze anxious as she approached.

"Unfortunately, no," Olivia replied, frustration creeping into her voice. "I'm still looking. No one seems to have any idea where she could be."

Jill's shoulders slumped in disappointment, the resolve she had been holding onto briefly slipping away.

"Thank you for everything you're doing," Jill murmured, her tone heavy with worry, before she turned and headed back into the crowd, visibly weighed down by the dog's absence.

Olivia took a deep breath, trying to steady her own rising anxiety. The rehearsal dinner was winding down; the chatter had lessened, and guests were drifting off in small clusters, their voices fading into the background. Olivia glanced around, noticing the flickering lights of the lanterns outside and the soft clinking of glasses as people wrapped up their conversations.

Olivia turned and spotted Katherine, engaged in animated conversation with a small group near the bar. Tulip, now back in her cage after her performance, squawked intermittently, her loud cries cutting through the otherwise quiet conversation like an uninvited guest.

Olivia moved through the crowd, glancing towards the exit as more guests departed.

"Hey, Katherine," Olivia called as she approached, trying to keep her voice light despite the tension curling in her chest. "I think I'll take Tulip back to the cottage. Is that okay?"

Katherine looked at her with a bright, almost too eager smile, as if she'd been waiting for the offer. "Oh, yes, of course! I'm sure Tulip will be much more comfortable there," she said, her voice a bit too cheery, almost as if she was relieved to be rid of the bird for a while. As Katherine handed her the bird's cage, she noticed a fleeting glance between Katherine and Monica across the room—quick, but sharp, a silent exchange that raised the hairs on the back of Olivia's neck.

"Are you sure everything's alright?" Olivia asked, studying Katherine more closely. Katherine's smile faltered for just a second, her posture stiffening before she masked it again.

"Of course," Katherine replied too quickly. "Just, you know, everything's a bit much with the wedding. But thank you for taking Tulip. You're a real help."

Olivia couldn't shake the feeling that something was left unsaid, but before she could ask more, Katherine excused herself and quickly returned to her group. The moment lingered in Olivia's mind, a sense that she had glimpsed something deeper, something hidden beneath the surface. As Olivia made her way back to the cottage with Elmer trotting beside her, her thoughts swirled, each additional detail from the evening refusing to fit into a clear picture. She was still reeling from everything she had observed when something caught her eye—Thomas, sitting on a bench in the garden. His pen moved across the pages of his notebook, his focus unbroken by the soft evening air around him.

As Olivia walked past, she didn't expect him to notice her, but just as she reached the path toward the cottage, Thomas stood up and approached her quickly, his sharp gaze locking onto hers. "Olivia, right?" His voice was direct, cutting through the evening air. "You're the one in charge of the animals? Chardonnay? Was she under your care when she went missing?" His question hit Olivia like a jolt. She wasn't sure if he was accusing her or just trying to get information. "Yes," she replied cautiously, her voice unintentionally defensive. She wasn't sure why he was asking or what he knew.

Thomas wasted no time. "I need to know what you've seen, what you've heard. You've been around, right? You've talked to people, you've noticed things. Who's acting strange?" His questions came quick, each one sharper than the last. He was probing her, trying to get to something deeper. Olivia shifted, a wave of uncertainty washing over her as she set Tulip's cage on the ground. She wasn't used to being on the other side of the interrogation. "I don't know what you mean," she said, her voice steady but unsure. Thomas took a small step closer, narrowing his eyes as though she were a puzzle he was trying to solve.

"You think it's a coincidence? The dog going missing, Desmond acting like he's got everything under control while his sister, Monica, does everything she can to distract from whatever they're really up to?" His voice lowered with each word, his eyes never leaving hers, as if daring her to acknowledge the weight of his words. Olivia's heart raced. She suspected something was off between Monica and Desmond, but the way Thomas was speaking made her wonder how much more was beneath the surface. "What are you getting at? I'm sure it's just wedding stress," Olivia replied, trying to keep her voice casual. She gestured toward the main house, attempting to dismiss the unease building in her chest.

Thomas gave her a dismissive glance. "Stress doesn't make people act like that. You're missing the point. Monica's the one pulling the strings—Desmond's just the face of it all. This whole wedding—it's part of something bigger, something they've been working on for months."

Olivia felt a chill rush over her. "Something bigger? What are you talking about?" She had trouble wrapping her mind around the idea that something like a con could be at the heart of all this. His gaze flicked past her, scanning the shadows in the garden before locking back onto her. "Desmond's got the perfect persona—calm, collected, that squeaky-clean reputation. But Monica? She's the mastermind behind it all, steering things from the background. I don't know who she's after, but she's playing a dangerous game, and it's not just about Chardonnay."

Olivia's pulse quickened. *Was he suggesting that their connection to the missing dog was part of something calculated? That Desmond and Monica were using the wedding as a tool in a larger scheme?* "Are you saying they're behind Chardonnay's disappearance?" Her voice was quieter now, the weight of her question heavy in the air. Thomas's eyes darkened, the intensity of his stare almost too much to bear. "I don't have all the answers, but I know enough to tell you that all of this connects. The dog's disappearance? Just a piece of the puzzle. They're hiding something; if you continue to push, you might uncover something unpleasant."

Olivia felt a wave of dizziness wash over her. She wasn't sure if she should be scared or more determined to find the truth. Everything she thought she knew about the wedding—and the people in it—was now in question. "You're not making any sense," Olivia said, her voice trembling slightly, despite her best efforts to stay composed. "How do you know all of this?" Thomas's expression softened for a moment, but it wasn't a kind look. "I know what I've seen. I know how people act when they're hiding something. Desmond and Monica? They're hiding more than you realize."

A chill ran down Olivia's spine. *What was he not telling her? Was he just trying to scare her, or did he really know something she didn't?* Before she could respond, Thomas stepped back, his face slipping into an expressionless mask. "Just watch your back, Olivia," he warned, his voice low. "This whole thing's about to blow up. And when it does, you don't want to get caught in the fallout." Without waiting for a reply, Thomas turned and disappeared into the shadows, leaving Olivia standing in the garden, her thoughts spinning. Her instincts told her he wasn't lying, but his cryptic warnings only raised more questions than answers.

She stood frozen for a moment, not sure what to do next. *Was Thomas right? Were Desmond and Monica involved in something much darker than a simple wedding?* Olivia glanced down at Elmer, who had been waiting patiently by her side. He looked up at her with wide, unblinking eyes, as if he too could feel the weight of the mystery hanging in the air. She didn't know what to believe, but one thing was certain: she couldn't ignore the nagging feeling that something far more sinister was at play. And if she was going to uncover the truth, she needed to act fast before the pieces of this puzzle slipped out of her grasp.

As Olivia stepped into her cottage, she tried to push aside the weight of her thoughts. The quiet calm of the space contrasted with the storm raging in her mind. She paused for a moment, breathing in the stillness, but it did little to calm the unease tightening in her chest. Something was shifting, and she could feel it.

The other pets had already dozed off. Benny lay sprawled in the center of the floor, still half-engaged in a battle with his chew toy, completely oblivious to everything around him. Chester, ever the regal figure, lounged on the sofa, indifferent to the whirlwind of activity that had marked the day. Ayla lay in her plush dog bed, paws crossed, as though nothing could disturb her peace.

Elmer, ever the loyal companion, gave Olivia one last glance before trotting off toward the bedroom, his quiet steps barely audible on the hardwood floor. Olivia stood for a moment, taking in the sight, but it didn't bring her the comfort it should. The presence of the other animals—content and sound asleep—was a cruel reminder of the one who wasn't there. Chardonnay should've been curled up in her plush dog bed, safe and sound, dreaming of her moment in the spotlight tomorrow. Instead, she was out there, alone, somewhere in the dark, perhaps cold, scared, or worse. The thought twisted Olivia's gut, a pang of guilt lacing her every breath as she stood in the stillness of the room. Every sound, every peaceful movement from the animals, only made her more acutely aware of the missing piece. *How long could Chardonnay last like this? She wasn't accustomed to being on her own. How much longer until time ran out?*

She changed into her pajamas, the weight of the day bearing down on her. As she moved through the familiar motions, her mind raced—whispered secrets, knowing glances exchanged in corners, and the palpable tension that had followed her all evening. Despite her exhaustion, she knew sleep would remain just out of reach while questions swirled in her thoughts.

The wedding was tomorrow, but Chardonnay was still missing, and Olivia felt no closer to finding her than when she'd first disappeared. She couldn't shake the feeling that something was slipping through her fingers, that time was running out. She let out a long breath, trying to quiet the storm in her mind, but it wouldn't be silenced. The weight of everything—the uncertainty, the mounting pressure—pressed on her chest. She couldn't afford to let the questions go unanswered, not when so much was at stake. Eventually, exhaustion took over, and Olivia sank into bed, but her sleep was fitful, filled with restless tossing. The only thing that gave her any peace was the faint hope she was on the brink of uncovering something—something monumental—but she couldn't shake the fear that she might be too late.

CHAPTER 15

The morning of the wedding dawned crisp and clear, the fresh chill in the air highlighting the vibrant hues of nature around Dogwood Cottage. Olivia, still grappling with Chardonnay's disappearance, made her way toward the coffee bar, every step laden with urgency. The scent of dew-soaked grass mingled with the rich, inviting aroma of freshly brewed coffee, promising a brief reprieve from the chaos.

The scene around her felt like orchestrated chaos. Laughter rose from the garden as guests sipped coffee and enjoyed an elaborate breakfast buffet. The sound of their chatter swirled around Olivia, contrasting with the knot tightening in her stomach. Soft notes from a string quartet floated on the breeze, lending an elegant soundtrack to the frantic pace. Everywhere Olivia looked, something caught her attention—caterers arranging trays of hors d'oeuvres, bridesmaids adjusting their dresses, and guests chatting, all immersed in the whirl of pre-wedding preparations.

As she rounded the corner of the main house, Edward dashed by, nearly colliding with her, his arms full of an enormous floral arrangement that blocked his view. He muttered under his breath, face flushed with urgency. "Excuse me, sorry, just—almost there!" he said, brushing past her.

Olivia stifled a laugh as she brushed herself off and spotted Ashley behind the coffee bar.

Ashley was pouring coffee with her usual precision, her hair pulled back into a practical ponytail. Olivia and Ashley had been friends since high school, and even after all these years, Ashley had remained a steady presence in her life. She'd always been the one to offer a warm smile and a grounding sense of calm, even when everything around Olivia seemed to spiral.

When Olivia reached the coffee bar, Ashley didn't need to ask what she wanted. She simply handed her a steaming Styrofoam cup with her favorite latte. The warmth from the cup radiated through Olivia's fingers, offering momentary solace amid the wedding chaos.

"Morning, Olivia," Ashley greeted, her smile knowing, as if she could sense the weight of the past few days. "You look like you could use this."

Grateful, Olivia took a long sip, letting the bitter warmth spread through her chest. "You have no idea," she sighed, the comforting scent of cinnamon and coffee wrapping around her like a familiar hug.

"How's everything going here? Any new gossip from the guests?" Olivia asked, trying to shift her mind away from the missing dog and the unraveling tension.

Ashley leaned in closer, her voice dropping to a conspiratorial whisper. "Oh, you wouldn't believe what I've heard this morning." She glanced around, ensuring no one was eavesdropping before continuing. "Apparently, there's been some serious chatter about troubled finances—specifically, about Desmond's."

Olivia's interest piqued. "What kind of trouble?" she asked, furrowing her brow.

Before Ashley could respond, a burst of laughter echoed from a nearby group of guests, the sound jarring amid the tension that gripped Olivia. The wedding's joyful mood starkly contrasted her inner turmoil.

Ashley checked the crowd one more time, then spoke quickly. "Someone overheard a heated argument between Monica and Victor last night. Sounds like Monica's trying to close a deal, and she's got Desmond involved in securing Victor's participation. It's big—and not in a good way."

Olivia felt a sinking feeling. "Monica and Victor?" she repeated, trying to process the information. She'd suspected Victor was involved in something shady, but hearing that Desmond was also part of it made her stomach churn.

"Yeah," Ashley confirmed, her expression tight with concern. "It sounds like some kind of investment scam—maybe a Ponzi scheme. They roped Desmond into it, but I don't think he knows how deeply he's involved."

Olivia's thoughts raced as she took another sip of coffee. "Why would someone like Desmond get mixed up in something like that?" she wondered aloud. She couldn't reconcile the image of the upstanding groom with the possibility of him being tangled in a scam.

Ashley shook her head. "I don't know. But I heard Monica is holding something over him—something big. Maybe that's why he's been so on edge. She's got him doing whatever she wants."

A knot tightened in Olivia's stomach as the pieces started to fall into place. If Monica was manipulating Desmond, then Chardonnay's disappearance might not just be a distraction—it could be part of a much bigger plan. And if that was true, Olivia wasn't just up against a missing dog, she was diving into the heart of a conspiracy. *Was Desmond an unwilling pawn, or was he in on it?*

"Thanks, Ashley," Olivia said, her voice carrying a note of gratitude despite the storm of thoughts swirling in her mind. "That could really help."

She glanced out over the lawn. Guests mingled; but something felt amiss. One guest was conspicuously missing—Thomas. Olivia's brow furrowed. He hadn't missed a chance to be at the center of things all weekend, and after their tense encounter last night, she had expected him to be everywhere today, tying up loose ends for whatever story he was chasing. Yet, there was no sign of him.

Her mind raced. *Why wasn't Thomas around? Had he found something else? Was he already digging deeper into this mess?*

"I need to follow up on a few things," Olivia said, turning to leave. "If you think of anything else, let me know."

"You got it," Ashley replied, her tone warm with a hint of encouragement. "Good luck, Olivia. You'll need it."

As Olivia walked away, Ashley called after her. "Oh, and keep an eye on Katherine. She's been unnervingly chipper this morning—I don't know if she's wrangled that parrot into the wedding or not!"

Olivia flashed a wry smile, but her mind was already elsewhere. "I will. Thanks."

With her thoughts buzzing, Olivia reflected on Ashley's words. Though they had provided no simple answers, they pointed to a bigger picture—Monica's behavior, the tension between the siblings, and the general discomfort hanging over the wedding. It all matched Thomas' cryptic warning from last night.

She pushed the doubts aside and focused on the one thing driving her: Chardonnay. The missing dog. The web of deception. The wedding that now felt like a ticking time bomb.

With a renewed sense of urgency, Olivia made her way toward the guest cottages. She had no time to waste—Chardonnay was out there, and Olivia couldn't afford to lose focus.

As she neared the larger cottages, she surveyed the area. Ten spacious, luxurious cottages, only eight showing signs of life. She noted two were unaccounted for. Curiosity piqued, her heart quickened as she continued toward the row of cottages.

A creak from a door snapped her attention back to the task at hand. Rachel emerged from a cottage, absorbed in her phone conversation. Olivia ducked behind a nearby tree, watching as Rachel, oblivious to her presence, wandered up the hill.

"One down, nine to go," Olivia thought, marking the cottage in her mental list. She waited until Rachel was out of sight before slipping closer, her focus sharp, every sense alert.

Olivia approached the next cottage, her senses sharp. High-pitched singing floated through the air—"Somewhere Over the Rainbow." Only one person had that voice: Katherine, Tulip's owner. Olivia breathed a quiet sigh of relief.

The next cottage was eerily still. Olivia crept closer, her footsteps almost silent on the gravel path. She scanned for signs of life—no open doors, no cracked windows. *Typical,* she thought, frustration building.

A partially open curtain caught her eye as she was about to move on. She cupped her hands around her eyes, leaning in closer.

Inside, the room was a mess—designer heels, half-packed bags, and expensive dresses draped haphazardly. Monica's cottage, definitely. Olivia's gut confirmed it. She focused on a table in the center, piled high with papers—financial documents. Schemes, she thought, adrenaline kicking in. Her heart raced as she tried to decipher the numbers and charts. This was it. Jackpot.

But then hesitation hit. *Was she crossing a line? What if she was wrong? Was this worth the risk?*

Her thoughts churned, but her resolve solidified. She had to find out. Chardonnay's safety, the scheme—it all depended on uncovering the truth.

Taking a deep breath, she looked for a way in. She circled the cottage, eyes darting over windows and doors, searching for an entry point. Every choice felt risky.

Then she spotted it—the sliding glass door on the patio, ajar. A small gap. The break she needed.

Seriously? Sliding doors again? Olivia pushed the thought aside. She couldn't afford to second-guess now. Slipping her fingers into the gap, she nudged the door open just wide enough to slip inside. The air felt thick with uncertainty, but there was no turning back.

Inside, Olivia crouched low, her heart hammering. Her eyes scanned the room, darting over the scattered papers. A pamphlet labeled "Investment Prospectus" caught her eye. She flipped through it, her brow furrowed at the exaggerated promises—too good to be true. She snapped a photo hurriedly.

Next, her fingers skimmed a list of names—some marked with check marks. *Were these Monica's secured investors?* Seeing Victor's name made her stomach twist. The question mark beside "secured?" stood out. *Was she reading too much into this?* But it matched Ashley's warning: Victor was the deal she needed to close.

Her eyes slid over bank statements—erratic withdrawals and deposits, including one marked "Overdue." That didn't bode well. *Was this just mismanagement, or the key to the scheme?*

Then she spotted the manila folders, each filled with identical contracts, all waiting for signatures. One had Victor's name, but no signature. She set it aside and opened the next folder—promissory notes. Empty promises, the kind of paper Monica wasn't planning to honor.

Olivia's mind raced, connecting the dots between Ashley's and Thomas's words. *Manipulation? A scam just beginning to show itself?*

The last folder was empty, except for a sticky note: "D for T." Scrawled hastily. Desmond? But why was it empty? What did "T" mean? Her heart skipped. This was more than just a clue. She could feel it.

Her fingers brushed the edge of the manila folder, pushing it aside, and that's when her gaze landed on something else—a crumpled edge peeking out from underneath it. She pulled it free, her breath catching as she unfolded the corner of a faded newspaper article. Her eyes skimmed the headline, and her stomach dropped.

"Montgomery Family Plagued by Untimely Deaths in Fiery Crash—Authorities Suspect Foul Play."

Her pulse quickened. The article, over a decade old, detailed the mysterious deaths of Desmond and Monica's parents in a fiery car accident. The phrasing of the article was chilling. The words "suspected foul play" hit Olivia like a punch to the gut.

She scanned the article, but her mind was already racing, piecing together the timeline. *What was Thomas investigating, and how deep did this all go?*

Her fingers tightened around the paper as the realization hit her—Thomas had uncovered something much darker than just a financial scheme. As Jill had told her, the mystery of Desmond and Monica's parents had always been vague, and now Thomas might have found the answers.

Olivia quickly folded the article back up, slipping it into the folder. She needed to connect all the dots before this dangerous game spiraled any further.

A rustle outside froze her in place. *Footsteps? Voices?* Her pulse spiked. She pressed against the wall, her mind whirling. *Had anyone heard her? Was someone coming?*

Panicked thoughts swirled, but she focused. She couldn't afford to be caught. The room felt smaller, the air thicker, as the pressure mounted. *Who was "T," and why did this detail feel so crucial?*

Quickly, she snapped more photos, hands trembling, and retraced her steps to the door. The sticky note burned in her mind as she eased the door closed, barely breathing. Her heart pounded. *What was going on here?* This was bigger than she had imagined, and time was running out.

Olivia closed the door gently, her heart racing as she scanned the area for any sign of being seen. The quiet around the cottages felt out of place, a sharp contrast to the chaos of the wedding. *How had she ended up here?* She shook her head, hurrying down the path. This wasn't the life she'd imagined when she came back to Emerald Ridge—caught between a celebration and a dark mystery growing with each step.

The financial papers she'd just uncovered gave her a glimpse of the truth—just enough to know something was wrong, but not enough to understand it fully. And now, she had to return to the charade, pretending to be the cheerful pet-sitter, all while searching for answers.

Taking a steadying breath, Olivia headed back to the main event area. The crowd still lingered, drinks in hand, laughter bubbling in the air, but most of the bridal party had already retreated to prepare for the ceremony. Their idle chatter felt distant, muted by the urgency pulsing through her veins.

Monica, Desmond, and the growing whispers of fraud swirled in her mind—Ponzi scheme. She'd heard of them, of course, but they always seemed like the stuff of movies or TV. Not something that could touch her, let alone unfold right before her eyes. And yet, here she was—staring down the possibility that a much darker scheme unknowingly ensnared everyone around her, including the innocent.

CHAPTER 16

Olivia knew Ponzi schemes thrived on deception—promises of easy money, high returns, and an inevitable crash. But who was pulling the strings? Monica's control over Desmond seemed obvious, but were they just pawns? Or was the corruption deeper, reaching farther than she realized?

The financial documents hinted at something bigger, and the involvement of guests like Victor made Olivia question how deep it went. Her heart sank. *What kind of person willingly joined such a mess?* The risks were enormous, and some guests were likely caught up in it, oblivious to the impending fallout. *Were they duped into believing they were part of a legitimate investment?*

The more she thought about it, the more she realized how easily someone like Monica could pull off a scheme like this. All she had to do was charm people, hide her true intentions behind a well-manicured exterior, and make it seem like everything was legitimate. But the more Olivia uncovered, the more everything unraveled. The interactions between Monica and Desmond were only the beginning.

How many people here were unknowingly about to become victims? How many would wake up tomorrow with their lives shattered, trusting the wrong people? How many would even notice? Olivia had to figure it out—fast—before lives were ruined.

She checked her phone and was reminded of the next task on her list: gathering the dogs and escorting them to the groomer. As much as she wanted to keep chasing leads, she knew this next part was non-negotiable. Still, she sensed that even in this seemingly mundane task, she might uncover more or find a moment to think.

The dogs were both her responsibility and her excuse to blend in. But they also kept her from diving headfirst into the deeper mystery that was spiraling out of control.

After returning to the pet cottage, where Ayla, Benny, and Elmer waited for her, Olivia took a deep breath. "Alright, gang," she muttered, grabbing their leashes. "Time for your spa day."

In the circular driveway sat the grooming van, emblazoned with a colorful logo. Shana, the groomer, was leaning against the side of the van, arms crossed and a grin on her face. "Is this the four-legged bridal party I'm taking care of?" she teased.

"Yep," Olivia huffed, as Benny tried to make a break for it. "Think you can handle these three all at once?"

Shana laughed. "I'll give it my best shot. If anyone can make them wedding-ready, it's me." She gestured to the open van door. "Let's get this party started."

Benny was the first to go, wriggling furiously as Shana lifted him into a playpen inside the van. Ayla trotted in obediently, climbing right into the grooming tub like a seasoned pro. Elmer, however, required a bit more persuasion.

"Come on, buddy," Olivia coaxed, gently pushing him toward the van.

Elmer dug in his heels, glancing over his shoulder with a look of utter betrayal. "I know, I know. It's a travesty," Olivia muttered. "But it's for the wedding, okay?"

With a last nudge, Elmer reluctantly climbed into the van, flopping down dramatically in the back corner. His expression was one of resignation, as if he were a martyr in a bath towel.

Shana gave Olivia a wink. "This shouldn't take more than a couple of hours, assuming I survive."

Olivia laughed. "Good luck. Just text me when they're ready."

With the dogs in Shana's hands, Olivia found herself with some unexpected free time. The morning's discoveries and looming wedding still weighed on her mind. *What's my next move?*, she wondered.

As Olivia rounded the corner toward the pet cottage, she nearly collided with Noah, who was walking in the opposite direction.

"Hey Liv!" he called, flashing a grin.

"Hey, Noah! Where are you off to?" she asked, catching her breath.

"Just taking a quick stroll to clear my head," he said, then added with a curious tilt of his head, but Noah's expression sharpened with recognition.

"I've seen that face before," he remarked, a hint of concern creeping into his voice. "What have you gotten yourself into this time?"

Olivia sighed, "That's a loaded question.", she said with a chuckle.

Glancing back in the direction she'd come from, she told Noah. "I'm heading back to the cottage. Most of the pets are getting pampered by the groomer right now, so I have a little time."

"Have you found any clues about the missing dog?" Noah asked, his brow furrowed as he glanced around. "The wedding's only a few hours away, and I overheard a few guests chatting about it. I figured you were involved somehow."

"No," Olivia admitted, frustration clear in her voice. "No leads on her, but I found something else that might be important." She lowered her voice and looked around, making sure no one was in earshot. Then, without warning, she grabbed Noah's arm and started guiding him toward her cottage.

"Whoa, where are we going?" Noah asked, half-laughing, half-confused.

"Just come with me," Olivia said, her voice low and conspiratorial. "I've got something to show you."

Inside the pet cottage, Chester's unamused stare from his armchair and Tulip's disapproving squawk met them. Chester blinked at Noah, saying, *Who let this one in?*

"No love for new people, huh?" Noah said, eyeing the cat and bird.

Olivia smirked. "Consider it a rite of passage."

They sat on the couch, and Olivia pulled out her phone. Scrolling through the photos from Monica's cottage, she handed the phone to Noah. "Take a look."

Noah swiped through the images, his expression shifting from curiosity to concern. "How did you get these?"

"Don't ask," Olivia waved it off. "Do they look suspicious to you?"

Noah scratched his head, still staring at the screen. "Well, I'm no expert, but these high-return promises seem... dodgy. And if these are guest names, I'd say that's a big red flag."

"Exactly," Olivia nodded. "And it gets worse. Monica's Desmond's sister, and Victor's his business partner. I've seen Monica having some intense talks with both of them. It's definitely not about wedding flowers."

Noah's brows raised. "So, you think Monica's pulling Victor into some shady deal, and Desmond's somehow involved?"

"That's the vibe," Olivia said, leaning back on the couch. "But why would Desmond risk his entire career? It doesn't make sense."

"Maybe Monica's holding something over him," Noah suggested. "Leverage?"

"Maybe," Olivia sighed, frustrated. "But where does Chardonnay fit in? Was the dog just a distraction, or is there more to this?"

Noah ran a hand through his hair. "Liv, I get it, but maybe you're overthinking. Rich people do weird stuff with their money all the time. This could blow up on its own. Just find the dog and let the rest play out."

Olivia's gaze hardened. "I can't just walk away. What if I can stop something bad from happening?"

Noah's concern deepened. He hesitated, then spoke softly, "I just worry about you, okay? You're a good—friend—and I don't want anything bad to happen to you."

Olivia's chest fluttered at the unspoken words, but she pushed it aside. "I'll be careful. But I can't ignore it."

Her phone chimed, breaking the moment. She glanced at the screen and smiled. "Looks like the dogs are ready. Want to come help me pick them up?"

Noah's face lit up with a smile. "Sure, I'll help."

They stood, the serious moment easing into camaraderie as they headed toward the front of the venue to collect the freshly groomed dogs.

When Olivia and Noah arrived at the grooming van, a frazzled Shana cigarette dangling from her lips met them. Her hair was a mess, and she looked like she'd just survived a battle.

"Everything go okay?" Olivia asked, keeping her tone light.

Shana shot her a deadpan look. "You kidding? I don't get paid enough for this. Got the job done, but I think I burned enough calories to skip the gym for a month. Three at once? Big mistake."

Olivia and Noah exchanged a knowing glance. Shana stubbed out her cigarette with a muttered curse. "Alright, let's get them."

She slid open the van door, revealing the three freshly groomed dogs. Benny was the first to tumble out, his floral bowtie already askew. He bounced down with enthusiasm before rolling in the dirt.

"No, no, Benny!" Olivia groaned, biting back laughter.

Shana closed her eyes, resigned. "Should've seen that coming."

Ayla followed, her regal air undisturbed by the chaos. Her coat shimmered in the sunlight, a delicate wreath of flowers crowning her head.

"Now that's a model dog," Noah said, impressed.

Finally, Elmer shuffled out, his floral collar and pinned flowers betraying his humiliation. His squinting eyes practically screamed "discomfort."

"Jill wanted him to get the full treatment," Shana shrugged. "So... here he is."

Olivia and Noah snorted in laughter, struggling to keep straight faces.

"Thanks, Shana," Olivia managed, still holding back a giggle. "Let's get these guys back to the cottage before they ruin any more of your hard work."

Elmer led the way down the hill, his stride exaggeratedly slow, as if the weight of his flower garland was too much to bear. But as they neared the cottage, he quickened his pace, eager to escape any onlookers.

"You look handsome, Elmer," Olivia said, trying to soothe him. "It's only for a little while. As soon as your part is done, I'll take it all off."

Elmer let out an exaggerated sigh. *Not talking to you,* he grumbled in Olivia's mind. *I smell like flowers. I smell like FLOWERS. What do you think I am, a walking bouquet?*

Olivia bit back a laugh. "I'm not his favorite person right now," she whispered to Noah, trying to suppress her amusement. "Hopefully, he'll forgive me by dinnertime."

Noah chuckled. "He's got a point, though. It's not exactly his brand."

At the cottage, Olivia released the dogs. Ayla settled into her bed, careful not to smash her crown. Olivia tried to dust off Benny's now dirt-covered bow tie, but as soon as she freed him from his constraints, he began zooming around the room, a continual blur of motion.

Elmer, however, slunk into the far corner, wedging himself between the bed and the wall. He turned his back to the world, letting out a dramatic sigh. *I'll just be over here,* he thought, as if the floral collar was a personal betrayal.

Noah glanced at Olivia. "I've got one last check on the Rolls before the ceremony. Let me know if you need anything, alright? And try not to get into too much trouble."

Olivia flashed him a grin. "I'll do my best."

As the door closed behind him, Olivia surveyed the room—Benny zooming, Ayla's crown still intact, and Elmer sulking in the corner. She sighed.

Time for a plan.

The mystery notes Thomas had been taking, Monica's schemes, and Chardonnay's disappearance were all tangled together. She had to fit the pieces together before the wedding started.

A sense of determination settled over her. There was work to do, and she wasn't backing down until it was done.

CHAPTER 17

Olivia moved quickly back toward the guest cottages, heart pounding with anticipation. Each step grew heavier as her thoughts raced; she had to find something concrete—something that could tie all the threads of this mystery together before the wedding began. Distant sounds of last-minute preparations—the murmur of voices, the clink of glasses, the rustle of decorations being adjusted—charged the air. With every passing moment, the urgency wove itself tighter around her.

Only a couple of cottages remained unaccounted for, and she suspected one of them belonged to Thomas. With a racing pulse, Olivia approached the cottage across from Monica's. She listened, straining to hear anything out of the ordinary. There was nothing—no voices or footsteps disrupting the peace, just the chirping of birds and the gentle rustle of leaves in the soft breeze. *Perfect*, she mused, a semblance of hope blooming within her.

The front window was slightly ajar, and Olivia stared, incredulous. *Seriously? This place is less secure than a cardboard box.* Adrenaline kicked in. She pushed the window wider, wriggling onto the sill. Her entrance was anything but graceful; she fell, landing face-first on the sofa.

Shaking off the impact, she muttered, "So much for a stealthy break-in."

Olivia scanned the cottage, searching for any signs of life. It was similar to hers, yet far more luxurious; plush seating, a small wall table, and a rear bedroom. Then her eyes landed on the leather notebook on the coffee table. *Thomas's.* The one he'd been scribbling in all weekend.

This is it, Olivia thought, her resolve hardening as she moved toward it.

Olivia flipped open the notebook with urgency, her eyes scanning the frantic scribbles. Desmond's background, Monica's strange behavior, potential scandals—it was all here, a jumble of revelations that felt almost too much to process at once. This wasn't just rumors, this was real.

A sound from the cottage's rear froze her — unmistakable footsteps, then running water. *Oh God, Thomas is here!* Panic surged as she flipped through the notebook faster, her eyes darting over phrases like "Desmond's double life," "Monica's pressure tactics," and "possible blackmail."

Her fingers fumbled as she flipped through the pages, finding several folded documents hidden between the sheets. She pulled them free with shaking hands. The first was Desmond's bar exam results—at a glance, they seemed legitimate. But something wasn't right. She squinted at the document. The testing center name was in a different font, starkly contrasting the rest of the document. Her breath quickened as she scanned the page more closely. Misspelled words. Typos. It wasn't just careless—it was rushed. Sloppy. A forgery.

Olivia's hands trembled as she stared at the documents. The inconsistencies screamed at her, but she needed confirmation. She fumbled to pull out her phone, typing into the search bar. She quickly checked several links, searching for matching documents.

Her stomach turned as she pulled up an image of real bar exam results. She compared the font and the layout. She glanced back at the one in her hand—completely different. It wasn't just the fonts; the layout itself was wrong. No official seal. No official markers.

Her heart raced. These weren't legitimate.

She checked the other document—Desmond's bar association certificate. The same glaring discrepancies: mismatched fonts, the seal all wrong. The realization hit her like an icy wave, undeniable.

She stepped back, the weight of it all settling over her. Monica had been holding onto this evidence to control

Desmond. Desmond wasn't a real lawyer. Her world seemed to tilt with the weight of the revelation.

Desmond had been living a lie. His career, his reputation—it was all built on fraud. Frantically, she reviewed Thomas's notes, searching for connections. Her eyes flew over the scribbles: "pressure from family," "Monica's manipulations," "forged documents." And then there it was. The key detail. Monica had given Thomas the forged copies of the bar exam and bar association documents. It all clicked into place. Desmond had never passed the bar.

Desmond's family, particularly his powerful lawyer father, had pushed him to this point. The pressure had crushed him, leaving him tangled in a massive lie. Olivia's mind raced as she read further—mentions of a mysterious law school friend, someone complicit in the deception, helping to prop up Desmond's lawyer facade and cover up the truth.

Olivia's stomach churned. What she was uncovering was bigger than just a wedding scam—it was a web of lies, manipulation, and betrayal that reached much farther than she could've imagined. Olivia snapped pictures of the crucial notes with her phone. A sudden tension gripped her, the urgency of the situation dawning on her. She needed to get out before Thomas finished his shower.

With adrenaline spiking, she grabbed the documents, her pulse pounding in her ears as she prepared to leave.

She moved swiftly, slipping through the door as quietly as possible.

Once outside, Olivia pressed her back against the cool cottage wall, taking a moment to catch her breath. Her heart still raced, but a small grin tugged at her lips. *Got it,* she thought, the thrill of discovery pushing her forward.

As she moved toward the last row of larger guest cottages, her surroundings were quiet—everyone was likely busy with last-minute preparations for the big event. She rounded the corner of the last cottage when a low growl shattered the silence, followed by Monica's sharp voice cutting through the air. "Shut up, you mongrel!"

Olivia's heart leaped, a jolt of adrenaline rushing through her veins. That exact phrase Tulip had repeated back at the pet cottage. She crept closer, ducking behind a bush near the front door, hoping to hear what was happening inside. One of the cottage windows stood slightly open, and she strained to catch Monica's voice drifting out.

"Ugh, I can't wait for this day to be over," Monica lamented. "You'll go back to your owner, and I'll close my deal. If not, well, I'm not sure what I'll do with you."

A shuffling sound followed by the creak of the cottage's front door set Olivia on edge. Monica was leaving. Olivia held her breath, every muscle tensed as she waited for the sound of footsteps to fade, her ears straining for any sign that Monica was lingering nearby. The sounds of the cottage—the faint hum of the wind through the window, the rustling of leaves—were deafening in the silence.

"Please be here," Olivia thought, praying the door wasn't locked. She reached for the handle, her fingers trembling as they made contact with the cold metal heart thundering in her chest. The door resisted for a moment, then with a soft click, it popped open. *Thank you, universe,* she thought, flooded with relief.

Slipping inside, Olivia closed the door gently. The cottage was dark, save for the minimal light filtering through the windows. The air was stale. This cottage obviously hadn't served as guest accommodations for a while. The faint but unmistakable odor of mildew and dust clogging her senses. The faint mustiness in the air clung to her skin as she hurried through the gloom, her breath coming shallow and quick.

A growl cut through the silence, the deep, guttural sound urging her forward. Olivia's pulse spiked. She rounded the corner and found a small bedroom, the space cold and oppressive. There, lying on the floor, was Chardonnay—exhausted, her fur matted, and her body curled protectively around the rusted chain that held her. Her spirit was battered, but the sight of her made Olivia's heart leap.

Chardonnay's tail gave a weak thump as Olivia kneeled beside her, and the sound sent a wave of relief crashing over her. "Oh, Chardonnay," Olivia whispered, her voice thick with emotion. "It's okay, girl. I'm here."

The poodle sniffed Olivia's hand weakly before settling her head back onto the floor, too tired to react. Olivia's heart twisted in her chest as she saw how different this was from the comfortable life Chardonnay knew. The harsh reality of the chain was a stark contrast to her usual pampered existence. A link, rusted and worn, stood out like a beacon. Olivia's thoughts raced—breaking it would require more than just strength.

I need a tool, she thought, her mind snapping into focus as she scanned the barren room. The emptiness mirrored her desperation, and the only things in the room besides Chardonnay were a bowl of dry kibble and an empty water dish. Her eyes fell on something outside the window—a large, flat rock. She darted out the door, grabbed the rock, and rushed back inside.

"Okay, girl," Olivia whispered, trying to keep her voice calm. "Let's try this."

Her breath came in quick, controlled bursts as she gripped the rock. She slammed it down on the rusty link, the sound of metal hitting stone filling the air. It barely moved. Chardonnay flinched at the noise, pulling back in alarm, her eyes wide with confusion and fear.

"Hang in there," she urged, her voice trembling as she tried again. But the link didn't budge.

Frustration bubbled up, hot and sharp. In her pocket, she felt the treats she had used earlier for Ayla and Benny, and guilt washed over her. She didn't want to do this, but it was her only choice. She placed the treat just out of Chardonnay's reach, her stomach twisting with the unfairness of it.

"Come on, girl, you can do it," Olivia whispered, her voice soft but urgent.

The scent of the treat filled the air, and Chardonnay's eyes locked onto it. Olivia could see the flicker of life return in her—her determination sparked by the promise of the treat. The poodle strained against the chain, trying to lunge forward. The link tightened around the pipe; the tension growing with each pull. Desperate, Olivia pounded the chain, each blow stronger than the last.

Come on, come on...

With a resounding crack, the chain snapped free just as Chardonnay lunged for the treat. The relief hit Olivia like a wave, her breath coming out in a sharp gasp as she let herself exhale.

"Yes!" she whispered, her voice breaking with the weight of the moment. "Good girl!"

Chardonnay looked up at her, a look of trust mixed with the remnants of her ordeal. As she chewed on the treat, Olivia fashioned a makeshift leash from a rope she found in the corner. "Sorry, girl," she muttered, her voice filled with apologies. "This will have to do for now."

As she led Chardonnay out of the cottage, her mind raced. With the dog safe, a weight lifted from her shoulders. But this was only one piece of the puzzle. The storm was building, and Olivia knew she had no time to waste.

With urgency, Olivia sent a quick text to Shana, the groomer, her pulse racing with every second.

Olivia: *Are you still here?*

Shana: *Yeah, Jill asked me to hang around in case there were any last-minute grooming needs.*

Olivia: *Perfect. I found the missing dog. I'm bringing her over now. She needs the same treatment Elmer got.*

Shana: *Copy that.*

Olivia saw the time and felt a pang of anxiety;a little over an hour before the ceremony. Gently tugging on the leash, she encouraged Chardonnay to follow her. The poodle moved slow and steady, her spirit kindling a bit as they made their way up the hill and around the far side of the venue, strategically avoiding the main paths crowded with guests.

Miraculously, they reached Shana's grooming van without being spotted. Shana opened the door, her eyes widening in surprise. "I have so many questions," she said, glancing at the frazzled pooch.

"I know, but first, we need to get her clean and presentable," Olivia urged, urgency threading her voice.

Shana nodded, taking the rope from Olivia and leading Chardonnay into the van. While Olivia jogged back toward the pet cottage, her mind spun with thoughts of the documents she had discovered. If she was going to solve this mystery, it had to be now—before her prime suspects vanished into the chaos of wedding festivities.

CHAPTER 18

Olivia glanced toward the ceremony site perched atop the hill. Her heart raced. Final preparations were underway, and she knew minutes were slipping away to solve the mystery unraveling around her.

Olivia's eyes locked onto the reception tent, a flurry of activity as the staff made last-minute adjustments. But it wasn't the frantic pace that drew her attention—it was Monica. Standing just outside, her posture rigid, Monica surveyed the scene with an intensity that made Olivia pause. She gripped her phone tightly in one hand, and an irritated frown marred her face. She was waiting for someone—someone who was clearly late.

A knot of unease twisted in Olivia's gut. She hesitated, watching Monica for a few more moments, her mind racing with possibilities. Monica was always so poised, so in control. But this—this wasn't her usual polished demeanor. Olivia lingered in the cottage's shadow, hoping to blend into the background.

The minutes dragged on. Olivia's pulse quickened as her instincts screamed at her to stay alert. It wasn't long before Victor appeared, walking up to Monica with an air of hesitation. Their exchange was strained, measured.

Monica's movements were fluid, practiced—she flicked her wrist, and Olivia's heart lurched as she saw the papers slide from her designer handbag. Documents. A set of them. Monica's fingers gripped them tightly, her posture leaning forward as if she were handing over a secret she was desperate to keep. She shoved the papers into Victor's hands with a swift, almost too eager motion.

Victor hesitated, his gaze flicking between Monica and the papers. The pen in his hand hovered above the page, his fingers twitching, but he couldn't quite bring himself to sign. Olivia's stomach twisted as she watched, every instinct on high alert. She couldn't hear their words, but the air crackled with unspoken tension. Monica's every movement seemed calculated—her body language screaming urgency and control. She leaned in close, her voice low and honeyed, but the way her fingers brushed Victor's arm sent a shiver up Olivia's spine. There was something possessive in her touch, something dark.

And then it hit Olivia—the realization slammed into her chest like a freight train. This wasn't just a casual exchange. This was *the* deal. These weren't just any papers; these were the final documents—the ones that would seal the financial deal Monica had been working. She watched, breath caught in her throat, as Victor's eyes flicked over the papers, his hand trembling before he slipped the pen back into his pocket. Victor handed the papers back to Monica, shaking his head, his face hardening with an emotion Olivia couldn't read. Without a word, he turned on his heel, practically fleeing the scene, his pace quickening as if he couldn't escape fast enough.

Olivia's eyes flicked to Monica, and the sight of her was like a spark to dry tinder. Rage twisted across Monica's face, hot and sharp. She hadn't sealed the deal. With a furious jerk, she shoved the papers back into her purse and pulled out her phone, her fingers flying over the screen with a speed that spoke to her frustration and desperation.

As Olivia tried to process the gravity of what she had witnessed, her phone made a loud noise—a barking dog, echoing through the otherwise quiet garden, loud enough to make Monica's head snap in Olivia's direction. The tone for her text messages. Olivia froze, panic rising in her chest as she shrank back against the wall. Monica's eyes scanned the area, her gaze narrowing as she searched for the source.

Olivia held her breath, praying Monica wouldn't spot her. Monica's gaze lingered a moment longer before she turned, papers in hand, heading back towards the guest cottages.

Her heart pounded as she glanced at her phone screen to see whose message had arrived.

Shana: *Pretty, pretty princess is ready to go.*
Olivia: *On my way.*

Olivia shoved her phone back into her pocket and made her way back toward the grooming van. With a new leash in hand, Shana smiled as she met her at the door. "Hope you don't mind. I traded the rope for something more appropriate," she chuckled.

Olivia smiled, her heart lightening as she saw Chardonnay peeking out from behind the door, visibly revitalized. Shana gently tugged, and Chardonnay trotted out, looking like her old self—pristine once again, though Olivia could still see the lingering anxiety etched into her expression. Cautiously, the poodle stepped out of the van, glancing around as if something sinister might jump out at her at any moment.

Olivia's heart ached for the dog. Despite being the most spoiled dog she had ever met, Chardonnay did not deserve the stress she had faced in the past day. Leaning down, she stroked the poodle's back, now silky soft and smelling of flowers. "It's okay, girl. The worst is over. Let's get you back to Jill."

Grateful once more, Olivia thanked Shana before heading off to the main cottage, Chardonnay in tow, excited to return the beloved dog to her rightful owner just in time for the wedding.

Olivia and Chardonnay climbed the polished wooden stairs of Dogwood Cottage, the sunlight streaming through the large windows and casting warm patterns on the floor. The scent of freshly pressed linens and flowers filled the air, causing a blend of excitement and apprehension in Olivia's stomach. With a tentative hand, she tapped on the door; the sound echoing in the hushed corridor.

"What?" came a sharp reply from within, the tone laden with stress. "I swear, if I wanted to do everything myself, I wouldn't have hired you people."

Olivia paused, her heart racing as she heard hurried footsteps shuffling toward the door. Suddenly, the door swung open, revealing Jill in a white silk robe embroidered with the word "Bride," her hair wrapped in a fluffy towel. A forced smile plastered across her face faltered at seeing Olivia. "Oh, Olivia, it's just you. I thought you were one of those inept assistants who has been bothering me all morning..." Her voice trailed off as she caught sight of Chardonnay patiently sitting beside Olivia, her tail thumping against the floor in a show of excitement.

"Oh, my gosh! Olivia, you found her!" Jill exclaimed, falling to her knees in front of Chardonnay, enveloping the dog in a tight embrace. The poodle's eyes sparkled with joy, nuzzling into Jill's embrace as tears pooled in the bride's eyes. "My sweet girl! I'm so glad you are okay." Jill pulled back, scrutinizing Chardonnay's fur. "And you're clean?" she asked, a flicker of concern weaving through her words.

"It's a long story," Olivia began, her voice echoing the gravity of the moment. "I'll tell you all about it later, but right now, we've got Chardonnay back, and you both need to get ready for your big day."

In a whirlwind of emotion, Jill threw her arms around Olivia, who froze, unsure how to respond to the overzealous gratitude. "Thank you so much, Olivia! This is the best wedding present ever."

Olivia managed a chuckle as she extricated herself from the embrace, feeling warmth wash over her. Chardonnay had already crossed the room to the plush dog bed by the window, and was snoozing blissfully, leash still attached. "Oh, and Jill," she ventured, her voice steady but serious, "just so you know, I'm not 100 percent sure what all happened to her. She seems mostly unharmed, but she's been a little out of it. I'm hoping if it's some kind of sedative, it will work its way out of her system soon, but you might want to let her sleep as long as possible."

Jill's expression shifted from concern to anger, her eyes widening. "Some monster drugged my dog? I swear, if I find out who did this..." She glanced over at Chardonnay, still peacefully dreaming, then back at Olivia, determination igniting in her gaze. "Thank you again for everything, and I will take your advice to let her get her beauty sleep."

Olivia nodded, feeling an ache of responsibility. She moved toward the door, as Jill muttered under her breath, "If I ever find out who did this..." As she descended the stairs, Olivia grimaced at the thought brewing in her mind—someone Jill cared about was far closer to the truth than she thought, and probably one of the last people she would ever expect.

Pushing open the back door of the main house, Olivia hurried towards the pet cottage, the sun warming her back as butterflies flitted from bloom to bloom in the garden around her. She needed to get dressed and make sure Ayla and Benny were in their places on time.

As she pushed the door open, the scent of freshly washed dogs enveloped her, making her smile. The room was peaceful. Ayla was snoozing in the plush dog bed by the window, her crown of flowers untouched. Benny lay sprawled out in the middle of the room, a puddle of drool collecting by his mouth, while his bowtie lay abandoned across the floor, looking worse for wear beneath the bedside table. Tulip and Chester monitored the scene from their perches, sharing a silent look of disdain for each other.

Then there was Elmer, sound asleep, sprawled across the bed, deciding comfort outweighed his pouting. Olivia's entrance barely stirred anyone from their serene states. She knew, though, her next words would draw Elmer's focus.

"Hey, Elmer!" Olivia called, her voice light and cheerful. Elmer lifted his head, blinking at her as if awakening from a dream. "Guess what, bud? You're off the hook for the wedding! We found Chardonnay!"

At this revelation, Elmer sat up, ears at attention, eyes sparkling as his tail started an enthusiastic wag. He flopped over and began rolling around on the bed, presumably to rid himself of that 'clean' smell, plunging into joyous abandon. The sight made Olivia burst into laughter, an involuntary response to his exuberance.

"Don't get too excited, though! You still have to go to the wedding, just as an observer, not a participant." With a resigned huff, Elmer plopped his head back down, yet his tail kept wagging.

Fine by me, she heard his thoughts echo in her mind, carefree and content. She glanced at the other sleeping pups, assessing her next move. Ayla was perfect as is, so no need to disturb her just yet, but Benny...

Olivia retrieved the bowtie from under the table and ambled over to Benny, hoping to reattach it without waking him. No such luck. As she bent to clasp the bowtie around his neck, Benny jolted awake, launching into a wild sprint around the room, tail wagging at lightning speed.

"Oh, for heaven's sake!" she sighed, laughing as she tried valiantly to block and catch him. Eventually, Olivia surrendered, flopping down onto the floor with a soft thud. Almost instantly, Benny zoomed over, flumping down in front of her on his back, legs in the air and tail wagging with unrelenting enthusiasm.

With ease, Olivia clasped his bowtie around his neck without a hint of resistance. Once she was done, he immediately curled up in her lap, panting with joy, flashing her an exaggerated doggie smile that could melt even the iciest heart. *That must be it*, Olivia thought, glancing down at the little troublemaker. *If you're on your feet, he thinks it's time for chase; but if you sit down, he realizes it's time to calm down.*

As she stroked his soft fur, soaking up the rare calm radiating from him, Elmer's thoughts drifted into her mind, tinged with amusement. *Took you that long to figure that out? I thought you were good with animals.*

Olivia narrowed her eyes at Elmer, who was giving her a smug look from the bed. "Well, if you knew, why didn't you say something?" she asked, her voice holding an edge of irritation.

Elmer's expression transformed into a doggie smirk, his tail thumping against the bed's surface. *It was more fun to watch you chase him.*

With a sigh, Olivia shook her head at his antics. "Glad I could entertain you," she shot back. Standing, she scooped Benny up and set him in one of the unused dog beds. "Keep these guys out of trouble; I've got to get ready for this wedding."

With her dress in tow and her bathroom bag slung over her shoulder, she marched into the bathroom.

Thirty minutes later, Olivia emerged, transformed. Her hair and makeup were perfectly done, and her soft peach dress, ethereal against her skin, fluttered around her knees. Elmer blinked at her a few times, his head tilting comically as he let a thought slip. *Pretty.*

She smiled, warmth blooming in her chest. "Thanks, bud," she responded, though she wondered how long her 'pretty' appearance would last when trying to corral three dogs at a wedding ceremony. Rarely did she dress up or play with her hair and makeup, and while it felt nice, a hint of discomfort lingered.

"Come on, guys! We have a wedding to attend!" she declared, addressing the animals in the room. Ayla sat primly at attention, her gaze steadfast, waiting to be leashed. Benny zoomed in circles around her ankles, a whirlwind of excitement, while Elmer made it clear he wasn't budging from the bed until it was 100 percent time to go.

Turning to the two pets who wouldn't be joining the wedding festivities, she told Tulip, "Your services aren't needed today, okay?" The parrot immediately launched into a rendition of "Somewhere Over the Rainbow," impressively off-key. *Right, those services,* thought Olivia. After the rehearsal disaster, Jill decided walking a cat down the aisle wasn't the best idea, much to Seth's relief. Olivia turned to Chester and said, "And you just behave, okay?" Chester blinked at her, as if to say that doing anything else was preposterous.

Leashes clipped securely to the collars of Ayla, Benny, and Elmer, Olivia pushed open the cottage door, her heart racing with anticipation. *Game time,* she thought, as they made their way up the hill toward the ceremony site.

CHAPTER 19

Olivia's steps slowed as she approached the wedding site. The lush green lawn of Dogwood Cottage stretched out before her, framed by towering mountains in the distance. Pristine rows of white chairs and the large ivory arch, draped with soft pink peonies and white roses, were impeccably arranged. The delicate scent of flowers mingled with the fresh-cut grass beneath her feet, creating an intoxicating atmosphere that seemed both magical and unsettling.

She glanced at the flawless arrangement—*how many hands had it taken to achieve such perfection? Was there a precise measurement for each chair?* Her mind wandered, but before she could focus on anything specific, a gentle breeze rustled the dogwood trees, sending petals fluttering to the ground like soft confetti.

As she moved deeper into the scene, the sound of the bubbling fountain to her right added a calming tone to the air. It seemed as if someone had carved the entire wedding from a dream—everything perfectly in place. Olivia's mind drifted to the thought of her own wedding, should she ever have one. *Would she create an elegant wedding, or would she let laughter and spontaneity lead the way?* The image of Noah in a black tuxedo, standing at the end of a wedding aisle, flashed in her mind. Startled, she quickly shook her head, a faint smile tugging at her lips. Her thoughts were venturing into territory she wasn't ready to explore. It must've been the atmosphere of the wedding affecting her.

The thought faded as reality set back in. Olivia glanced toward the reception tent, where caterers scrambled to transfer a massive cake onto a crystal stand, while others bickered over the placement of mini éclairs. It was a reminder that even grand events have their flaws.

Olivia smiled to herself, appreciating the small human moments behind the curtain of perfection. As she looked around, wondering if the day would go off without a hitch or if surprises were waiting to emerge, she caught sight of Monica and Rachel overseeing the altar, their faces tight with tension.

Approaching Rachel with Benny and Ayla in tow, Olivia called out, "Hey, Rachel! These two have parts in the wedding, but I'm not sure where they need to go."

Rachel's smile broke through her stress as she bent down to scratch Benny's ears, her mood lifting instantly. "Hey, Benny boy! You've been good for Olivia, haven't you?" she cooed, earning a joyful spin from the pup.

Rachel stood, holding out her hand for the leashes. "I'll take them. I'm not sure where they're supposed to go, but maybe Monica knows..." Her eyes landed on Elmer. "What about him? Isn't he supposed to walk Jill down the aisle?"

Olivia paused, a smile tugging at her lips as she tried to contain her joy. "He's no longer needed." She left it at that, choosing not to explain the details of Chardonnay's return.

Rachel's surprise was apparent, but she nodded with understanding and took Benny and Ayla toward Monica. Olivia, relieved of two of her charges, took Elmer by the leash, moving toward the floral tent to stay out of the way of the wedding's shifting chaos. She'd wait there until it was time to take her seat.

Olivia peeked around the entrance flap of the floral tent, her heart fluttering with a mix of nerves and excitement. The air inside was thick with the rich, sweet aroma of blossoms, and her eyes landed on Edward, who was a whirlwind of motion. He reminded her of Monica at the altar—entirely absorbed in the chaos of last-minute arrangements, his brow furrowed and mouth set in a determined line. He pointed at various people with the precision of a traffic cop, urging them towards their designated tasks with a fervor that hinted at the pressure he was under. With the last large arrangements spirited out the flapping door, Edward's gaze met Olivia's.

"So, you're still swamped right up to the wire, huh?" she chuckled, stepping into the floral sanctuary, instantly enveloped by a cacophony of vibrant colors and the soft rustle of leaves.

Edward's dramatic shake of his head was almost theatrical. "I think we've finally got everything in place," he breathed, gesturing toward a nearby table. It groaned under the weight of a lavish bouquet of peonies, several smaller arrangements, and a few boutonnieres that looked as if they had sprung from a painter's palette. "Once I hand off these beauties, I can finally breathe and, well, watch the spectacle—I mean, the wedding—unfold."

Olivia smiled, relieved that she wasn't the only one feeling as though the wedding might spiral out of control at any moment. "What's brought you back here?" he inquired, his voice piercing through the ongoing clamor.

"Just trying to find a quiet corner to hide until ceremony time," she replied, motioning towards the frenetic energy outside the tent. "I'm afraid I'll get trampled by a rogue caterer or drafted into the floral brigade if I linger out there."

Edward chuckled, "Good call!" Meanwhile, Elmer, Olivia's steadfast companion, had already claimed his territory in a shadowy nook, flopping down and soon succumbing to a contented nap, his breathing softening into a rhythmic sigh.

Olivia noticed Edward's furrowed brow as he surveyed the arrangements and the leftover blossoms. "Everything alright?" she asked.

He sighed, half-smiling. "Yes, and no." He gestured toward a cluster of arrangements at the end of the table. "These were supposed to have a specific pop—a particular purple lily, but some of the lot I ordered... disappeared. There was enough to work with, but they're missing that wow factor. Jill insisted on including it because it was Monica and Desmond's mother's favorite flower."

"Disappeared?" Olivia asked, intrigued.

"Yeah. They were in large buckets of water in the back," Edward explained, his voice tinged with concern. "Yesterday, when I arrived, I found two buckets empty, and one knocked over." "You think they were misplaced?", asked Olivia.

Edward shook his head. "I really hope so. That lily's hard to find. It's not sold wholesale, and it's got some toxic properties. I'd hate to think something—or someone—got into them. It's beautiful, sure, but dangerous when ingested or handled for too long." He paused, glancing at the purple flowers. "I'm not sure what it says about someone when their favorite flower is so toxic," he added, raising an eyebrow.

"How dangerous?" Olivia asked, her curiosity piqued.

Edward hesitated, then shrugged. "Well, the flower's got sedative properties. In small doses, it can calm, but at the wrong dose, it can make someone very sick. If not flushed from the system quickly, it can slow the heart and breathing to dangerous levels." He paused, his tone serious. "It has a weird sweet flavor, too, apparently—though whoever figured that out probably didn't live to tell the tale. Jill insisted on having it."

Chardonnay came to Olivia's mind, recalling how drowsy the dog had seemed earlier. At first, she'd assumed it was from the trauma of being lost, but now... she wasn't so sure.

"If wildlife got into it, what would happen?" Olivia asked.

"With a few petals, most likely, just a nice nap," Edward said. He paused, the unspoken implication clear. "The thing is, there are no set dosages, which is why it's so tightly regulated," he continued. "The toxicity varies from plant to plant based on a lot of factors."

Olivia hesitated, then, with a quick breath, admitted, "I found Chardonnay."

Edward's eyes widened with cautious curiosity. "Where?"

"It's a long story," Olivia said, choosing not to go into details. "But when I found her, she was sedated. I thought it was just the trauma at first, but now..."

Edward stroked his chin thoughtfully, processing Olivia's words. "It's possible it could be from that plant. But if someone's using it outside of a floral arrangement, they'd need to know what they were doing. It's not common knowledge."

Nodding, Olivia recognized this was just another puzzle piece—another fragment of the larger mystery. Just then, Edward checked his watch, the urgency in his voice rising. "Oh no, I've got to run," he exclaimed, swiftly gathering the blossoms for the bridal party. "The bridal party is meeting inside the cottage in just a moment, and I need to get these handed out." With that, he hurried away, leaving Olivia and Elmer amidst the flurry of floral preparation, their next move hanging heavy in the air.

Moments later, the soft strains of orchestral music floated toward her. Olivia peeked out of the tent towards the ceremony site, taking in hundreds of guests milling about like colorful butterflies, flitting to find their seats. Turning to Elmer, who seemed oblivious to the chaos, she raised an eyebrow. "Looks like it's showtime. We better snag our seats."

As they neared the seating area, Olivia took in the buzz of excitement in the air—guests smoothing dresses and adjusting collars, their nervous energy palpable. Guests in elegant pastels mingled, the warm atmosphere charged with anticipation. Olivia couldn't help but smile as an older man adjusted his bowtie with military precision, while a group of women in floral dresses chattered nearby. One fanned herself dramatically, and Olivia stifled a laugh. Her gaze then fell on a young boy, his oversized tuxedo barely containing his boundless energy as he bounced around the rose bushes, wrestling with his bowtie. Olivia chuckled as his parents exchanged exasperated glances, silently passing the responsibility of chasing him down.

Elmer trotted happily at Olivia's side, soaking in the attention from passing guests, his tail wagging as people cooed and stroked his head. He was blissfully unaware of the surrounding frenzy, content with the simple joy of affection. But Olivia wasn't so easily distracted. Beneath the chatter and excitement of the wedding, there was an undercurrent of tension that she couldn't help but notice. A few guests wore smiles that didn't quite reach their eyes, their forced cheer betraying the pressure to maintain appearances. It all felt off, like a carefully crafted facade.

She shook her head, trying to focus on the present, but the weight of the information she'd uncovered loomed in her thoughts. *Nothing here was truly as it seemed*, she mused, the mystery still swirling in her mind. Maybe it was just her imagination, or maybe the sense of unease resulted from the secrets she was holding onto. The pieces of the puzzle were there, but how to fit them together? She knew she had to wait until after the ceremony to figure it out, but then what? What would she do with what she knew once the vows were exchanged?

Finding a seat near the back of the aisle, Olivia settled in, adjusting Elmer beside her as he claimed the space with a contented huff, his eyes half-closed in relaxed contentment. She forced herself to focus on the beauty of the moment—the delicate archway, the soft rustle of the guests settling into place, the peaceful hum of anticipation filling the air. But despite the picture-perfect scene before her, a gnawing unease tugged at her.

She couldn't shake the thought of Monica and what might happen when she found out Chardonnay was safe. What would Monica do? Olivia had seen how carefully she controlled everything around her. The thought of what might unfold if Monica sensed her plans slipping away—if she realized someone had gotten one step ahead—made Olivia's stomach tighten. She knew she couldn't let her guard down just yet. The ceremony was a temporary reprieve, a moment where things seemed calm, but once the wedding was over, the reality of the situation would hit full force.

The pre-processional music faded into silence, signaling the start of the ceremony. Desmond walked down the aisle, his demeanor less that of a love-struck groom and more like a man tackling a task he'd rather not do. He exchanged a quick handshake with the officiant before taking his place at the altar. The bridesmaids and groomsmen followed in a perfectly coordinated procession, but the real showstopper was Monica. She glided forward with Marco by her side; her steps poised, but there was something off about her—something almost mechanical in her movements, as though she were performing rather than experiencing the moment. Her smile, though flawless, was flat, and Olivia couldn't shake the feeling that Monica was keeping something tightly controlled beneath her polished exterior.

Next came the pets, starting with Ayla, the pit bull, who proudly carried her flower basket down the aisle, basking in the admiration of the guests. Benny, however, zigzagged down the aisle like a pinball, darting in all directions as he tried to catch up to Rachel. Their playful antics sparked laughter, lightening the mood. Behind them came the ring bearer, the young boy in the tuxedo she had seen earlier, clutching a tiny pillow with an air of seriousness that contrasted with his earlier playful energy.

Elmer nudged Olivia's leg, and she smiled at his quiet pride in avoiding the surrounding chaos. But a sudden yip snapped her attention back to the front. Rachel was standing near the end of the row, holding Benny's leash, her voice a mix of urgency and laughter. "I can't keep him up there!" she exclaimed, handing the leash to Olivia. At the altar, Ayla lay between Shara and the next bridesmaid, while Benny, now back in Olivia's care, sighed dramatically. "At least he's contained for now," Olivia mused, looping the leash over her wrist. The music came to a halt, and the crowd's anticipation rippled through the air. *Here comes the bride,* Olivia thought, as everyone sprang to their feet, the atmosphere crackling with expectation.

CHAPTER 20

A hush fell over the crowd as the heavy doors of the main estate swung open, revealing Jill in her full bridal beauty. The soft fabric of her gown shimmered like sunlight on water, while delicate curls framed her glowing face.

On one side, an older gentleman—likely her father—escorted her with pride, while on the other, she held the leash of her beloved poodle, Chardonnay. The dog, perfectly groomed, mirrored Jill's elegance, her coat sparkling in the light.

As Jill ascended the front steps, the crowd watched in rapt attention, their eyes fixed on the trio making their way across the dew-kissed lawn. Olivia glanced toward the altar before shifting her gaze to Monica, wondering if Monica had seen Jill's grand entrance. But Monica, engrossed in

inspecting her nails, seemed entirely detached, unaware of
the bride's moment.

Jill paused at the head of the aisle while the triumphant
strains of the bridal march filled the air, and one of
the other bridesmaids nudged Monica, hoping to direct
her attention back to the ceremony. A collective gasp,
followed by a chorus of "oohs" and "aahs," rippled
through the guests as they realized Chardonnay was with
Jill. Olivia observed the expressions on several faces in
the crowd—her assumptions confirmed. Those who had
been worried about the dog's disappearance were now
expressing their relief, while others seemed struck by
the surge of emotions that accompanied Jill's stunning
entrance.

Olivia's gaze shifted back to the altar, where Desmond
stood, eyebrows raised in surprise at the sight of the dog.
A small smirk played at the corner of his mouth, as if he
understood exactly what the poodle's return meant for
Monica. Olivia's pulse quickened, her thoughts already
racing. Monica's reaction, however, was far less subtle.
Olivia saw her face transform from disbelief to fear, then
a flash of barely contained rage—before returning to the
forced smile, rehearsed for the crowd.

A quiet laugh bubbled up inside Olivia, which she
stifled.

But she couldn't dwell on it now. She forced herself
to focus on Jill as she walked gracefully down the aisle;
the music swelling around her. The guests were rapt,

some wiping their eyes, others completely entranced by the bride's beauty. There was a somberness to the scene, a reverence in their silence, but Jill's radiance couldn't be denied. It was like the clouds parting for a moment of sunlight.

Olivia's attention flickered back to the front as Jill reached the altar. The older gentleman, presumably her father, shook Desmond's hand, but it was clear Desmond's focus was entirely on his bride. His gaze was full of awe, though there was something between them—something Olivia couldn't ignore. Jill's radiant smile, her every move trying to pull him into the love that filled the air, contrasted with Desmond's stiff posture. His attempt to match her energy failed, and Olivia sensed the heavy unspoken tension between them.

Then came the shift. Jill handed her bouquet to Monica, Chardonnay's leash in her other hand. Olivia watched as Monica took the leash, straightening up, her body language stiffening in a way that made Olivia's stomach churn. Chardonnay, too, reacted, laying down at Monica's feet in a rigid, guarded posture, keeping as much distance as the leash would allow. Olivia's stomach dropped—whatever trust had once existed between them was shattered. Chardonnay seemed to know it instinctively.

Olivia's focus sharpened as she kept watch, every movement unfolding in front of her like a puzzle piece clicking into place. When Jill and Desmond joined hands again, preparing for the next part of the ceremony, Olivia couldn't shake the suspicion that the true drama was still yet to come.

"Dearly Beloved," the officiant began, his voice warm, yet carrying a weight of its own. "We are gathered here today in the presence of God, friends, and family to witness the union of Jill Hastings and Desmond Montgomery."

As the crowd's attention fixed on the bride and groom, Olivia's gaze swept over the gathering. A knot tightened in her stomach as she scanned the guests, searching for a familiar face still absent—Thomas. *Had he slipped away before the ceremony? Was he biding his time, waiting for the perfect moment to strike, pen poised to capture the unfolding story?* As an investigative journalist, it seemed almost impossible he'd leave before the event was over.

Her heart sank further. When her eyes found Monica, she froze. Monica's expression remained unmoved, her mask of indifference a stark contrast to the sisterly affection she should have been showing. She stood rigid, almost cold. Not a trace of warmth for either Jill or Desmond.

The ceremony continued, but Olivia's attention wavered. She couldn't help but see the red patch on Monica's leg—the one she had seen at the rehearsal dinner. It was still visible beneath her dress, but now it was more pronounced, blotchy, and irritated. Monica had tried to cover it with makeup, but it was only somewhat successful.

The discoloration had spread, a sharp contrast to the perfect façade she always worked so hard to maintain. Olivia's mind raced with possibilities. She glanced at Katherine, who had a matching patch earlier in the weekend, though hers seemed to be fading, successfully covered by makeup. *What was going on with these two?*

Trying to focus on the ceremony again was futile. Her discoveries weighed more heavily on her with each passing moment. Her knee jiggled with nervous anticipation. The leashes bounced with each movement, drawing an annoyed huff from Elmer and a soft growl from Benny, who was curled beneath her chair.

Up at the altar, Jill and Desmond dutifully began exchanging vows, but Olivia had a nagging sense that neither was fully present in the moment. The air buzzed with potential, each second ticking away, threatening to expose deeper truths.

Glancing at the bridesmaids again, Olivia saw Monica stealing glances toward the guest cottages. *Was she just ready for this whole things to be over with so she could return to her room, or was there something more?* If she hadn't looked suspicious before, she did now. The way she shifted her focus away from the celebration and toward the cottages unsettled Olivia. *What could demand Monica's attention so desperately?*

As the couple exchanged rings, a wave of relief washed over Olivia—thank goodness the ceremony was almost over.

"Before I bless this union, let's take a moment to reflect on what the Bible tells us about marriage," the officiant announced, launching into a verse, his words flowing like a river.

Olivia dropped her head into her hands. Or possibly not. She sensed the collective restlessness that ebbed through the crowd, the yawns that were stifled, the whispers exchanged. Thankfully, the officiant seemed to pick up on their impatience and soon wrapped up his biblical discussion with a flourish.

"With the power vested in me by this state, I now pronounce you man and wife," he declared, his face beaming with pomp. "You may kiss the bride."

Desmond leaned in, pressing a gentle kiss to Jill's lips, the crowd erupting with applause and cheers of joy. The music shifted, ushering in the processional as Jill, Desmond and Chardonnay made their way back up the aisle, smiles plastered on their faces, embodying the perfect picture of a happy family.

But Olivia knew better. As the bridesmaids and groomsmen followed behind, she caught sight of Monica practically dragging Marco along with her, urgency etched in her features as if she was in a hurry to escape.

Then, before she lost sight of her, Shara caught Monica by the arm. "Don't go anywhere, Monica! We still have pictures to take."

Monica slowed to a stop, spinning around, the tension in her smile barely concealed. The guests drifted towards the reception area, mingling and chatting as the wedding party gathered for photos.

Olivia, with Elmer and Benny in tow, took a longer route around, her eyes darting to listen in on any snippets of conversation exchanged amongst the wedding party. Just as she passed behind Shara and Monica, she saw Shara crinkle her nose, making a face while peering at the back of Monica's leg.

"Couldn't get that rash covered up with makeup, huh?" Shara asked, concern knitting her brow.

"It looks fine," Monica snapped. "No one is taking pictures of the back of my legs, anyway." Her gaze flickered back toward the cottages, the urgency of her earlier demeanor creeping back. "But maybe...maybe I should go try to cover it up better before the pictures," she said with forced casualness.

But before she could make a move, the photographer called to the bridesmaids. "Doesn't look like you have time," Shara said, offering a reassuring smile.

As the group gathered for their official photos, Olivia made a beeline for the floral tent, hoping to find Edward still there. She burst through the tent flap and caught Edward mid-swig from a flask. His eyes widened in surprise, and he coughed as the liquid caught in his throat.

"Olivia!" he exclaimed, startled. He tried to tuck the flask away, but Olivia waved him off.

"You deserve a drink; don't mind me," she said as she approached. "I have a question."

Edward cleared his throat, his face turning serious. "Ah, sure. What's on your mind?"

"Have you seen any skin irritating plants around? I know there was some poison ivy near my cottage, but was curious if you had seen it anywhere else?," she asked, trying to remain casual.

A puzzled expression crossed Edward's face. "Now that you mention, I have seen it in a few places, possibly some poison oak too. And it's been near cottages which I found odd because if I had guests on my property, I wouldn't want to risk them getting into something like that."

"Check," she murmured under her breath, her gears turning.

Edward's face turned serious, concern flickering in his gaze. "Uh-oh, you have that look on your face—what are you thinking?"

Olivia sighed, trying to gather her thoughts. "There's just so much more to this wedding than high-class opulence—there's an entire mess hidden underneath this cover of sparkles and glam. But your confirmation of the poison ivy may have just helped me put some pieces together."

"That's rather cryptic," Edward said, his curiosity piqued. "Glad I could help... I think."

They stood in comfortable silence for a moment while Olivia organized her thoughts. Peering out the flaps of the floral tent, she saw that the wedding photos were winding down. Someone herded the bridal party toward the reception tent, and she saw Monica still trying to make a discreet exit, but each attempt failed.

This is probably my only chance, Olivia thought, her heart racing. "Thanks for the help, Edward; I gotta go." She tugged at the dogs' leashes to get them moving. "Come on, boys."

"Good luck!" Edward called after her, watching with a mix of concern and curiosity as she hurried away. Olivia scanned the crowd for Shara, making a beeline toward her to collect Ayla before heading back to the pet cottage.

Olivia hurried back to the pet cottage, shoving the door open and unclasping leashes. She checked on the other pets, heartened to find Tulip and Chester still separate but alive, continuing to ignore one another with alarming accuracy. Benny trotted over to the water dish, took a few long gulps, and then flopped down in the middle of the rug, disinterested and exhausted from trying to be a good boy all day.

Olivia glanced down at her dress, realizing she didn't have time to change—but she would feel better if she could confirm her suspicions before Monica slipped away from the wedding festivities. Elmer waited patiently by the door, watching her expectantly.

"What?" she asked him.

Are we going?, came his response, tail thumping.

"I need to go do something, but it's better if you stay here."

Fat chance, he replied, his wide-eyed innocence practically daring her.

Sighing, she relented. "Fine, you can come. But stealth mode, got it?"

Elmer's tail thudded against the floor—a silent affirmation of his agreement. With her loyal companion at her side, a renewed sense of determination surged within Olivia. Together, they were ready to tackle whatever mystery lay ahead.

CHAPTER 21

Olivia made her way back to the guest cottages, the sun filtering through the trees to create a dappled pattern on the path below her. Elmer trotted at her heels, his tail wagging with a gentle rhythm that matched her own pulse of determination. A hunch nagged at her—intuition so strong she couldn't ignore it. Olivia had to investigate the area around Monica's cottage, Katherine's cottage, and the cottage where Chardonnay was hidden. Her mind raced as she mentally ticked off each location on her list. She started with Monica's cottage, glancing around to make sure no one was nearby. Her breath came in shallow bursts as she slowly circled the property, her eyes scanning the ground for any sign of poison ivy. She examined every shady nook, every hidden corner where the plant might thrive, but after two full laps around the cottage, she found nothing.

"Nothing," she muttered under her breath, frustration building. "Shoot." She paused, staring at the quiet landscape around her, the tension in her chest rising. *Had she been wrong about Monica's rash?*

Shaking off the uncertainty, she turned toward Katherine's cottage. With Elmer trotting at her side, she quickened her pace down the path, her thoughts still tangled. Olivia searched the grounds, employing the same cautious method she'd used at Monica's cottage. The area seemed quieter, almost too serene, as if hiding something beneath its calm exterior. As she circled the porch, her eyes caught something—a single vine of poison ivy creeping along the wooden steps. It was low to the ground, hidden where it would be easy to bump into, especially when rushing up the steps or walking absentmindedly.

Olivia's brows furrowed as she knelt down for a closer look. "This doesn't make sense," she mused, a nagging doubt present. *Had the red patch on Monica's leg really just been an allergic reaction to something else?* Olivia had been so sure. But then, Katherine could have easily brushed against it without noticing. It could have been purely coincidental.

Dismissing the idea, Olivia and Elmer pressed forward, heading toward the cottage where Chardonnay was hidden. A new sense of urgency came over her now that she had a clue. As she approached the porch, her eyes scanned the area, and then—there it was. A cluster of poison ivy, its glossy leaves creeping from under the porch steps, exactly at the right height for someone to brush their leg against without realizing. Olivia's heart skipped a beat, and she couldn't help but smile to herself in quiet triumph.

"Yes!" she whispered under her breath, relief washing over her as she took in the sight. It was what she had been looking for—proof that Monica could have come into contact with the plant while holding Chardonnay hostage. Now, everything was falling into place. Olivia's thoughts swirled as she continued to observe the ivy, feeling a mix of triumph and growing unease.

A low growl from Elmer cut into Olivia's thoughts. She glanced down at him, noticing how his body had tensed. He crouched low, his eyes locked on Thomas's cottage.

"What is it, boy?" Olivia whispered, but Elmer didn't respond, only offering another guttural growl that vibrated in his chest.

Her pulse quickened. Following his gaze, she focused her eyes on where he was looking. The cottage stood silent in the growing dusk, but then she heard it—a rustling, a shuffle of feet. Voices, low and strained, slipped through the air. One was male, the other female, their words hushed but sharp, like they were trying to keep the conversation under control, yet the tension between them was undeniable. Olivia's heart stuttered in her chest. The growl had been a warning. Something wasn't right.

She took a slow breath, trying to steady herself. Elmer's instincts were never wrong. It wasn't just an argument—there was something deeper, more dangerous.

Cautiously, Olivia moved toward Thomas's cottage. The air was heavy, pressing against her skin like it carried the weight of an unspoken truth. The closer she got, the more the voices seemed to sharpen, the male voice growing louder and more urgent, the woman's voice sharp with frustration.

When she reached the cottage, she paused. The door was ajar. Something about the scene felt wrong, like the air itself was holding its breath. She crouched beside Elmer, both of them pressed against the cool stone of the corner, hidden from view. Their breaths were soft, synchronized as they listened.

Clearer now, the fragmented but intense words revealed an unmistakable undercurrent of anger. With each passing second, the tension in the air thickened.

In a low and menacing voice, the woman warned, "You'll regret messing with me."

"Do you really think you can keep this a secret?" the man's voice came back, breathless, almost strangled, as though the words were fighting to break free. "You think your investors won't catch on? They'll turn on you. They always do."

"If you keep your nose out of it, that's exactly what will happen," the woman replied coolly. "I needed you only in case Desmond wouldn't cooperate. Blackmail was the only reason I gave you that information. But now... you've pushed too far. Done too much digging." There was a tense pause before she added, her voice low and menacing, "The things you've uncovered can't get out."

A shaky laugh escaped the man, his voice thick with disbelief. "And who's gonna stop me?"

The woman's laugh was bitter, almost mocking. "Who says I haven't already?"

"What do you mean?" he asked, his voice shifting, anxiety creeping in.

"Haven't you been wondering why you feel so off?" The woman's voice was silk and steel. "Dizzy, sweaty, nauseous? Can't catch your breath?"

A tense silence followed before the man muttered, "It's just allergies. All the animals around here..."

"Are you sure?" The woman's voice slid through the air, cruel with amusement. "Perhaps it's something you took to help with those allergies?"

There was another long pause, then the man's breath hitched. "The tea... the one the other woman brought me this morning."

A burst of laughter broke from the woman, sharp and biting. "You are brilliant, aren't you?" she taunted. "Look, it probably won't kill you. Not this time. I just needed to make sure we're on the same page. No article. Got it? But you'll feel like hell for the next few hours. Long enough to miss the wedding festivities. Such a shame... I'm sure you were looking forward to the cake."

Olivia's stomach churned as the conversation registered. Her mind raced, but the sound of Elmer's low growl snapped her out of her thoughts. This couldn't wait.

With Elmer at her side, she bolted toward the door, shoving it open with a force that startled her. The air was thick with danger, but Olivia wasn't going to let this moment pass without action.

The sight that greeted Olivia left her breathless. Papers scattered across the table, a chair lay overturned, and a tipped cup stained some documents with a brownish liquid. Her stomach clenched. And standing before her, locked in a tense standoff, were Monica and Thomas. Monica had Thomas pressed against the wall, gripping his collar tight. His face was ashen, sweat slicking his skin.

"Monica, what are you doing?" Olivia's voice cut through the tension.

Monica snapped around, releasing Thomas's collar as if it were nothing. "Olivia! What are you doing here?" she demanded, eyes narrowing with barely concealed anger.

"I could ask you the same thing," Olivia retorted, her eyebrow arching. "I'm pretty sure the maid of honor has duties at the reception."

Monica's lips twisted into a slow smirk. "You're right," she said, turning to leave. "I should get going." But as she tried to push past, Elmer stepped into her path, his growl low and unwavering.

"Get your mutt out of my way!" Monica snapped.

Elmer didn't budge, his growl deepening as he advanced, inching closer until he forced Monica to retreat. Olivia stood firm, eyeing her with determination.

"You need to answer for what you did to Thomas and Chardonnay," Olivia said, her voice steady, but the underlying urgency was unmistakable.

Monica scoffed, dismissing her with a flick of her hand. "What are you talking about? You think I did something wrong? Chardonnay's fine, and—" she motioned to Thomas, "—he's still breathing. What's the big deal?"

Olivia's jaw clenched. "He's not okay."

Monica chuckled. "Good luck proving I had anything to do with it. Perhaps it's food poisoning." Olivia followed her gaze, the pieces suddenly snapping into place. Sitting in a vase on the table were the toxic lilies Edward had warned her about, and Monica had mentioned doing something to his tea.

Olivia pointed to the flowers. "It shouldn't be that hard, considering the poison's sitting right there."

Monica's face twisted into mock surprise. "What? Those flowers? I don't know where they came from. In fact, I think Katherine brought him the tea. So, who's to say I'm involved?" She fixed Olivia with a challenging stare.

Olivia's eyes narrowed. "I heard the entire conversation, Monica."

Monica's smile faltered for a second, but she quickly masked it, shrugging. "I don't know what you think you heard. Thomas and I were just discussing an agreement. You're not a part of that." Her laugh was cold, condescending. "Besides, you think anyone here is going to believe you over me? You're a pet sitter, for God's sake."

Elmer, sensing the shift, stepped forward with a low growl, positioning himself between Olivia and Monica.

Before Olivia could respond, a loud crash broke the tension. She whirled around just in time to see Thomas crumple to the floor, retching violently beside a small trashcan.

Monica's casual laugh echoed in the space. "Do you believe I'd allow a reporter and a pet sitter to spoil my plans? Please." She stepped closer to Olivia, her voice dropping into a dangerous whisper, dripping with arrogance. "I know how to handle things. How to move pieces around on the board." She leaned in even closer. "And anyone who thinks they can take me down clearly doesn't know who they're dealing with."

Olivia's anger flared, but she forced herself to keep her voice steady. "You think you can do whatever you want and not face any consequences?"

Monica rolled her eyes, flicking her hair back with a dramatic flourish. "Sweetheart, I've been playing this game a lot longer than you. I know how to dodge bullets and come out on top. Besides,"—she gestured at Thomas, now gasping for air on the floor — "I'm pretty sure I've convinced him to keep whatever he's uncovered to himself. I've avoided consequences this long, no reason to take them on now."

A surge of determination rose in Olivia's chest. "This isn't a game, Monica! People are getting hurt, and you're toying with their lives!"

Monica's lips curled into a cold smile, and her voice dropped to a chilling whisper. "You have no idea how many lives I've played with." She stepped closer, her eyes locking onto Olivia's. "Don't preach the moral high ground to me. This is business. Sometimes, you do what you have to do to protect what's yours." Her gaze hardened, and she leaned in, her tone turning icy. "Just like with my parents. If I hadn't 'played with their lives, Desmond would have taken the entire inheritance. I couldn't let that happen. And Thomas? He was a loose end."

Olivia's heart skipped. The pieces of the puzzle were falling into place, but the weight of what she was hearing made her stomach churn. "What about your parents?" she asked, her voice barely above a whisper, almost dreading the reply.

Monica gave a dismissive roll of her eyes, as though it were the most obvious thing in the world. She turned toward the table, grabbing the newspaper article Olivia had seen earlier. Monica waved it under Olivia's nose. "Suspicions of foul play?" she taunted, her voice dripping with derision, as she tossed the article back onto the table.

Olivia remained silent, but her pulse quickened as she waited for Monica to continue.

Just then, another agonized retch from Thomas cut through the tension. Monica glanced down at him, unfazed, her expression almost bored, before turning back to Olivia. "It doesn't matter," she muttered, almost to herself. Then, with a sharp intake of breath, she began her story.

CHAPTER 22

"The pieces still aren't coming together for you, are they?" Monica asked with a sigh, her voice dripping with exasperation. She gestured toward the lilies on the table, a twisted smirk playing at her lips. "Those were my mother's favorite flower. My father sent them to her for every occasion—birthdays, anniversaries. But my parents were always very adamant about Desmond and I not touching them. As kids, we didn't understand why."

She laughed bitterly, her gaze distant as she relived the memory. "One time, when Desmond was about five, he ate one of the leaves. He got so sick, we had to rush him to the emergency room because my parents thought he was dying." Monica shook her head as if the thought were laughable. "Anyway, as I grew older, I started to wonder why those flowers were off-limits. I did some research and discovered that they were toxic. What does that say about my mom, huh? Keeping toxic flowers in a house full of children?" She tutted, the words pouring from her like venom. "But I was always the curious one. I figured out how much it took to knock her out, and I'd sneak it into her tea—her and my dad's tea—before bed. Made it a lot easier to slip out when they were passed out."

She turned her intense gaze on Olivia, her eyes cold. "Do you see where this is going now?"

Olivia's stomach twisted, but she nodded, her body tensing as Monica's smile grew darker, more malevolent.

"Anyway, my parents always loved Desmond more than me. I was never good enough. I overheard them one evening discussing their estate, how they were leaving everything to him because he was the 'responsible' one." Monica's face contorted with disgust. "They had an appointment to update their will the next day, and I knew I needed to do something if I was going to get my fair share." She shrugged, her tone almost casual. "My parents had some wine with dinner, and luckily, their anniversary had just passed. I knew how much of the lily would knock them out, so I figured if I tripled the dose, it would have a... different effect."

She leaned in closer to Olivia, the twisted satisfaction in her voice sending a chill down Olivia's spine. "I ground up the leaves and put them in their wine. It dissolves so easily. They ate, drank, then left to meet some friends. The magic of the flower kicked in, and dear daddy drove them full speed into a concrete barrier." Monica sighed as if remembering a fond moment. "By the time the paperwork came through for the estate, I got my half and Desmond got the other. Naturally, I helped myself to a portion of his, too. Handbags are expensive these days." She paused, twirling one of the lilies in her fingers. "And that's why I need this deal with Victor to work. That money only went so far."

Olivia's mind was reeling. She clenched her fists, stepping forward. "You think you can cover your tracks and walk away unscathed?" Her voice shook with anger, but she forced it steady. "You're cornered. Eventually, the truth will come out."

Monica's laugh echoed in the room, cold and mocking. "Please. I'm untouchable. I've made it this long, haven't I? And it's not like you have any proof. It's your word against mine. Who's going to believe you? You're just a small-town girl trying to play detective."

Olivia's pulse quickened, but she stayed calm, refusing to let Monica see her slip. "You may think you're clever, but you'll slip up. The truth always comes out."

Monica's smirk didn't falter. She took a step closer, her voice dropping to a chilling whisper. "Let me put it this way, Olivia," she said, her eyes narrowing. "You've already lost. I always win. And now? You're just putting a target on your back."

With that, Monica turned and shoved past Olivia, tossing the lily onto the floor. She strutted toward the reception, her smugness radiating from her like a poisonous cloud.

Olivia stood frozen, her eyes falling on the papers scattered across the table. Her mind was already spinning, connecting the dots, but the weight of the mystery pressed down on her. Everything—every piece of this tangled web—was connected.

Thomas groaned, the sound barely rising above a whisper, his body limp next to the trash can.

"Thomas?" Olivia's voice trembled with urgency as she crouched beside him. Fear curled in her stomach, its weight familiar and heavy. His head lifted weakly, but he collapsed back onto the floor, his skin a sickly shade of pale.

"What happened?" she asked, her voice steady but tight with concern. She already knew, but she needed him to tell her—needed his version to confirm Monica's cryptic words about Katherine and the tea. Answers, anything, to make sense of this spiraling mess.

"Bridesmaid," he rasped, the word hanging in the air, thick with meaning. Olivia's brow furrowed.

"Which one?" She leaned closer, every instinct demanding more.

He barely moved, offering a small, painful shrug that seemed to sap what little strength he had left. Her frustration boiled, but Olivia stood, scanning the small kitchen for something—anything—to help. Her eyes fell on a bottle of water on the counter. Without hesitation, she snatched it up and rushed back to his side.

"Here," she murmured, pressing the bottle to his lips. "Sip slowly."

His trembling hands fumbled for the bottle, draining it almost greedily, as if he were trying to quench the desert that had settled in his throat. When he finished, she set the bottle aside; her gaze never leaving his strained face.

"What did the bridesmaid do?" she asked again, her voice soft but insistent.

"Tea," he breathed. His words came in broken pieces, as though every breath took effort. "All the animals... allergies..." He grimaced, barely able to finish. "One of the bridesmaids... brought tea this morning." His eyes flickered, confusion clouding his already hazy thoughts.

"Who?" Olivia pushed. She needed clarity, fast. Her mind was racing, already spinning the threads into a tangled web.

He grimaced again, as though the question itself pained him, but finally muttered, "Blonde... high-pitched voice."

It didn't take long for Olivia to connect the dots. Katherine. The blonde bridesmaid who seemed to be everywhere, her bubbly exterior hiding something unsettling. If she was the one who brought the poisoned tea... why? Was she part of Monica's schemes, or had she been coerced into this? Olivia's gaze flicked to the purple lilies on the table.

"Where did those come from?" she asked, her voice quiet but urgent.

Thomas followed her gaze, then turned his bleary eyes back to her, struggling to focus. Slowly, he said, "Thought it was decoration."

Olivia's stomach churned. Monica must have placed them in the room before Thomas arrived. He probably hadn't even noticed, but the flowers were part of the poison. Exposure all weekend, and now the effects were clear.

Quickly, she grabbed another bottle of water, setting it beside him. "Stay here," she said gently, trying to sound more confident than she felt. "I'm going to... fix this."

Olivia's heart pounded in her chest, a knot of uncertainty twisting in her stomach. She had no simple answers, no plan—just an overwhelming sense that she couldn't walk away from the mess she had uncovered. *What could she do? How could she fix any of this?* She didn't know, but doing nothing was not a choice.

"Elmer, go find Noah," she commanded, her voice firm despite the anxiety that churned inside her. The dog's ears perked, and without hesitation, he darted out the door, his tail wagging furiously. Olivia's mind reeled with everything she'd learned—too many questions left unanswered, and too many people—Monica, Katherine, Thomas, tangled up in something she could barely begin to untangle.

One thing was certain: she couldn't back down now.

The realization hit her like an icy wave. Monica was right. She had no proof. *Who would believe such a wild story coming from her?* She'd sound like a lunatic, and the more she considered it, the more hopeless it seemed.

But then her phone buzzed in her bag, cutting through her spiraling thoughts. She fumbled with it, pulling it out just in time to hear the words, "voicemail ended." Her pulse quickened. Scrolling back, her heart leapt as she realized she had unknowingly dialed Noah while speaking with Monica. She must have accidentally hit the button when she was talking to her.

She checked the time the call had started—*had it recorded everything? The conversation with Monica? Could this be the proof she needed?* A rush of hope surged through her, so strong it almost made her dizzy.

"We need to get you some help," Olivia muttered under her breath as she dialed 911. The dispatcher's voice came through calm and efficient as Olivia explained the situation and gave her the address to the estate. The dispatcher confirmed help would be on the way soon. As she hung up, Elmer burst through the door, Noah following close behind, caught up in the dog's determination.

Elmer sat proudly next to Olivia, wagging his tail like he'd just completed a magnificent feat. "Good boy," Olivia praised, reaching down to pet him, momentarily distracted by his obvious pride.

Noah, looking a bit confused, raised an eyebrow. "I ran into Elmer on the path. I don't have your... abilities," he said, gesturing at the dog, "but it was pretty clear he was trying to lead me somewhere." He paused, looking between Olivia and Thomas, who was lying on the floor, clutching his stomach. "I saw you called earlier. Sorry I missed it—"

"It's fine," Olivia interrupted, her voice tight with urgency. "Just don't delete the voicemail I left you." She barely had time to focus on Noah before another groan from Thomas snapped her back to the situation at hand.

"So, what's going on here?" Noah asked, his eyes moving between Olivia and Thomas. The worry in his voice made Olivia's chest tighten.

"Remember all that stuff we talked about earlier?" Olivia began taking a steadying breath. "It's that, and a whole lot more." She paused, meeting his gaze, her thoughts gathering. "There's a blackmail and financial fraud situation, but also... this is Thomas, the reporter I mentioned." She gestured to the man on the floor. "He's been poisoned."

Noah's face darkened with concern, but Olivia could see the practical side of him taking charge. She couldn't waste any more time thinking. She needed to take action.

"Can you stay with Thomas until emergency services get here?" she asked, her voice steady, even though her insides were in turmoil.

Noah nodded, sinking to the floor beside Thomas, checking his condition as Olivia's mind raced with the next steps.

Olivia hesitated for just a moment, then remembered something. She turned back to Noah. "Noah, I need your phone." He looked at her, confused, but pulled it from his pocket.

"I need the voicemail I left you," she blurted, the urgency thick in her voice. "You can use mine for anything else." She thrust her phone into his hands without waiting for a response. Noah just nodded, slipping her phone into his pocket. The weight of the situation hanging in the air between them.

She turned back to Elmer, who was now sitting proudly at her feet, his head tilted as if he was ready for the next mission. "You're the best boy, you know that?" Olivia said, ruffling his fur and pulling him into a quick hug. Elmer responded with a smug, *I know.*

"Alright then," Olivia said, standing up straighter, the anxiety giving way to resolve. "We've got a mystery to untangle." With Elmer at her side, her heart steady and her purpose clear, she marched toward the door and headed up the hill to the reception, her mind focused, her steps resolute.

CHapTer 23

Olivia's shoes crunched against the gravel as she climbed the hill toward the reception, each step a physical reminder of the weight of the situation pressing down on her. Her heart thudded, the familiar anxiety mixing with a sharpened determination. The tangled web she had uncovered spun tighter with each passing moment, and she could feel it—one wrong move, and the whole thing might come crashing down like a house of cards.

She scanned the crowd as she neared the reception, her eyes flicking over the guests mingling in their elegant attire, their laughter ringing in the air, so detached from the chaos brewing beneath the surface. Despite the festive atmosphere, Olivia couldn't ignore the pit forming in her stomach. The pieces were falling into place, but she still didn't have all the answers.

Her gaze settled on Katherine. She was standing with the other bridesmaids, animatedly chatting, her laughter bright and carefree, as if nothing at all was wrong. Olivia's jaw tightened. There was no time for small talk anymore. It was time for answers. With her pulse quickening, Olivia's steps quickened as well. Her resolve sharpened—she wasn't going to let any more time slip away. This had to end now.

Without hesitation, she marched straight toward Katherine, cutting through the sea of guests with one goal in mind. She grabbed Katherine by the arm and yanked her away from the group, ignoring the surprised protests from the others. Katherine's face twisted in shock, but Olivia's grip was firm, unyielding. The sound of chatter behind her faded as Olivia focused on the woman before her.

"Oh, Olivia! Is everything okay with Tulip?" Katherine's voice was thick with concern. "Yeah, Tulip's fine," Olivia snapped, her eyes burning with urgency as she cut her off. "But Thomas isn't." Katherine's face drained of color in an instant. "Who? What do you mean?" she asked, her voice small. "Thomas—the reporter. The one who's been here all weekend." Olivia's words were like an accusation, heavy with gravity. She didn't wait for Katherine to process. "Why did you give him poisoned tea this morning?"

Katherine froze. Her eyes widened with panic, and her mouth opened, but no words came out at first. Olivia didn't let up, her stare unyielding. "Poisoned?"

Katherine stammered, her voice breaking. "I—I just gave him tea. I didn't—I didn't do anything wrong." Olivia's gaze softened just a fraction, her instincts telling her that Katherine wasn't capable of malice. But that didn't change the gravity of the situation. "Katherine, what happened? Why would you give him poisoned tea?"

Katherine stepped back, glancing nervously around the tent, her eyes darting as if she were looking for an escape that wasn't there. "I... I didn't know!" she whispered, her voice trembling. "Monica told me to deliver it. She said Thomas was having trouble with allergies from all the animals and wanted something to help him sleep. I thought it was just... just like an allergy pill. I didn't know it would..." Her voice cracked, and she swallowed hard, the weight of her unintentional mistake sinking in. "I didn't know it could hurt him."

Olivia's stomach twisted into a knot, the pit of dread deepening. *Monica.* The realization hit her like a punch to the gut. Monica had used Katherine as a pawn to carry out her plans. Katherine's face softened with guilt, her hands shaking as she clutched at her chest. "I didn't want to hurt anyone," she said in a whisper, her voice breaking. "Please, Olivia, you have to believe me." Olivia exhaled, her anger shifting into understanding. She could see the fear in Katherine's eyes. She wasn't the one to blame here. Monica was. "I believe you, Katherine," Olivia said, her voice full of compassion, though the fire still burned within her. "You're not the one we need to worry about."

Katherine's face relaxed, her shoulders sagging with relief. She nodded, grateful for Olivia's words, even though they solved nothing. Olivia turned away, her gaze sweeping over the crowd again. There, near the center of the tent, Monica was slipping into a conversation, a smug, almost victorious smile curling at the corners of her lips. Olivia's pulse quickened. Monica was too calm, too composed. Olivia was unsure who to approach first—Desmond? Jill? There were so many people involved in this mess, and she was no closer to knowing how to untangle it. But the one thing she was certain of was that Monica was at the center of it all, and she was going to expose her. No more running. Olivia paced for a few tense minutes, trying to make sense of it all. Every moment felt like a ticking clock, the pressure mounting as she realized how much was at stake.

Suddenly, Elmer's low growl broke through her thoughts. His fur bristled, a ripple of tension running through him as he shifted from his usual calm composure. Olivia turned to him, a question in her eyes. Elmer fixed his gaze on Monica, tracking her movements across the room with unwavering focus. He gave a low, almost inaudible whuff, like a quiet warning. Olivia's breath hitched. She knew Elmer had a way of sensing emotions, picking up on things that others couldn't. Olivia nodded at Elmer, a silent affirmation that they had to move forward. With renewed resolve, she pushed through the crowd, her steps swift and purposeful. The web was tightening, and she wasn't about to let it ensnare anyone else. The time for waiting was over. It was time to confront Monica.

Olivia and Elmer entered the reception tent from the side near the DJ booth. Monica stood in the midst of the reception, surrounded by guests but somehow managing to exude a sense of superiority that made Olivia's blood boil. A smugness radiated off her, like a foul smell clinging to her skin. *She really thinks she's untouchable,* Olivia thought, frustration simmering beneath her calm exterior. As if sensing Olivia's agitation, Elmer let out a small, dissatisfied growl beside her. "I know," Olivia murmured, pressing her lips together. "I know."

Olivia's gaze then shifted to Jill, the bride, who was floating gracefully through the crowd. Her reception dress was sleek and stunning, contrasting with the overwhelming glamor of her wedding gown. She moved from group to group, laughing and chatting, while Desmond lingered nearby, in and out of conversations with her, but always slipping away into deeper, more secretive discussions with Victor and Marco. Chardonnay, meanwhile, sat in a plush pet bed, watching the scene unfold with weary eyes. But something caught Olivia's attention. A brief exchange between Monica and Desmond. The look on Desmond's face—tired, almost resigned. Desmond stood near the bar talking with Victor. She leaned in closer, trying to hear what they were saying.

"I understand she's your sister, and everything looks good on paper, but the deal feels wrong. The prospectus is a little too sunny. I've been in business long enough to know that money doesn't work like that. I'm happy to sign the papers with Monica, but I need more information from her clients, or at least some insight into how things have been going. That can't happen tonight. I need more time."

Desmond's frustration was apparent, but he tried to hide it. "Got it," he muttered, turning his focus back to the reception. "Victor, you don't understand. Monica needs this signed tonight. If you sign now, you'll have a better chance of turning a profit than if you wait. Monica's leaving the country on Monday. There's no time after that." Victor drained his glass and scoffed. "If she's leaving the country, that gives me plenty of time to look into things further. You say the deal's urgent, but if it's a good deal, it'll hold for longer. She can leave the papers with you, and I'll sign them when I'm ready. You're a lawyer, right? You can witness the signing." Desmond looked defeated, his shoulders sagging under the weight of the conversation. Victor continued, "I'm not signing anything until I'm ready." He turned to walk away, but not before throwing Desmond a pointed look. "You'll see. A rushed deal isn't a good deal."

Desmond stood there, his gaze lost, and the tension was palpable. Monica, however, would not let it slide. She stalked over to him; her face a mask of determination, her hand gripping his sleeve and yanking him to the side. "What was that all about?" Monica hissed, her voice low with venom. Desmond looked down at his shoes, overwhelmed. "Victor's not ready to make the deal," he muttered, his tone defeated.

Monica's eyes narrowed dangerously. "And why isn't Victor ready to make the deal?" Desmond sighed, throwing his hands up in frustration. "He needs more time. Monica, I told you he would not be an easy sell. You can't just push someone like Victor around. He's too sharp. He needs to feel secure about this deal, and right now, he doesn't." Monica's eyes darkened, and she stepped even closer to Desmond, her face inches from his. "Fine," she spat, her voice full of ice. "You know what this means, right?" Desmond looked tired, resigned. "Yes. Do what you have to do. I'll deal with the fallout." Monica's lips curled into a tight smile as she let go of Desmond's sleeve. She turned away, brushing past him, but not without giving him one last, mocking look. "You don't get it, do you, Desmond? You never will."

Olivia's mind replayed the conversation between Monica and Desmond, her thoughts spinning with more questions than answers. The words "do what you have to do" echoed in her head, heavy with meaning. Had Monica meant that regarding Desmond's fake lawyer status? She'd already gone to great lengths to make sure Thomas wouldn't expose the truth—poisoning him to make sure he stayed silent. But the way Monica had spoken to Desmond... it was clear she wasn't revealing her full hand.

She was perfectly happy to watch him face the music alone. The more Olivia thought about it, the more everything seemed to fall into place—Monica had been playing a dangerous game with everyone involved. Desmond was in deep, possibly even deeper than he realized, and Monica wasn't about to let him escape unscathed. Whatever had been simmering between them was far from over. Olivia's gaze drifted back to Desmond, caught in the struggle between maintaining control and watching his world unravel. Monica's hold on him was undeniable, and she appeared to understand precisely how to maintain everyone near her off-balance. A sudden thought struck Olivia—*did Desmond even know what Monica had done to their parents?*

Olivia's stomach twisted with unease. *How far was Monica willing to go to protect her secrets? And how many more people—like Thomas—had she already manipulated, or worse, harmed?* The weight of it all pressed down on Olivia. She couldn't let Monica continue playing everyone like puppets. Not without exposing the truth. But first, she needed to make sure she had all the facts.

CHAPTER 24

As the resigned words left his mouth, Desmond glanced to the side and looked startled. Jill had wandered toward the conversation, clearly having overheard a significant portion of what was said. Her eyes widened, confusion spreading across her features.

"Uh, Desmond, dear, what is she talking about? What are you talking about? What fallout?" Desmond opened and closed his mouth a few times, like a fish out of water, not knowing where to start.

"Uh, Jill, it's not how it sounds. It's, uh, not that bad, I swear. It's just—" Desmond stammered.

Monica cut in, her tone dripping with rage. "Oh, Jill, it is as bad as it sounds, much worse, in fact." Monica's voice grew louder with each word, catching the attention of nearby guests who turned to witness the confrontation.

"You see, Jill, my dear, Desmond is a fake. A fraud. That's right, a complete fraud. You know how he's supposed to be this high-powered, rich lawyer? He's not. Not on his own accord. Law school, the LSAT, and the bar exam—he failed them all. He forged all his documentation. He knows enough about the law to keep himself afloat, but his boy Marco here,"—Monica swung her arm dramatically to gesture at Marco, who looked mortified — "is the one who does all the work; the real legal powerhouse. He's the one who does all the heavy lifting and tells Desmond what to say and do. Marco is the actual the legal genius, and I'm not sure why he's kept this backseat position to Desmond for so long."

Several gasps rippled through the crowd, and it dawned on Olivia that this was in part because many guests were Desmond's clients. Desmond hung his head in shame, the weight of his sister's words settling heavily over the gathering.

"Oh, and did Desmond tell you about our 'family money' and how he could pay for the whole wedding? There's no money, Jill. Desmond and I used it all on...other things. He's just as broke as all these people you hired to work for you," she said, gesturing around the room at the various wedding staff. Several looked up at Monica, clearly offended.

"Desmond, is this true?" Jill asked, her eyes pleading with him to prove Monica wrong.

Desmond let out a heavy sigh, throwing his arms up in the air. "Yes, Jill, everything Monica is saying is true. I'm a fraud."

He turned, facing the assembled guests. "You heard it here first, folks! I'm not a real lawyer; I just play one in the courtroom." He gestured at Marco. "But Marco here is a legit attorney and a good one at that, so if you need legal representation against me or anyone else, reach out to him. Obviously, I won't be of use to you anymore."

He suddenly turned, glaring at his sister with spite. He grabbed Monica's arm and pulled her toward the center of the dance floor, holding her arm in the air. "Before any of you leave, there is one more minor detail I need to mention. Apparently, fraud is a family tradition."

"My beautiful baby sister here has a lot of you duped as well. I am aware many of you have invested sizeable sums of money with her under a very sunny prospectus, looking forward to ample returns coming down the line. Monica has brought you all into a Ponzi scheme! Not only will you not be receiving any return on your investments, but you've been funding her extravagant vacations, her love for designer shoes, and her expensive taste in wine."

Monica's face froze, her jaw dropping in disbelief as her brother spoke. The crowd hung on every word, a mixture of shock and outrage filling the air.

Desmond continued, relentless. "She's as much of a fraud!—"

Abruptly, a police officer walked up between them, cutting off his tirade. "She's also an attempted murderer," the officer announced as he clamped cuffs on Monica's wrists.

Monica's mouth opened wider, if that was even possible, as she was cuffed. The rage that washed over her features was unmistakable. "He's a liar! A liar, I tell you! I would never treat my clients that way. Your finances are my top priority…

The officers were cuffing Desmond as well.

"Save it, sis, it's over," he said, shaking his head.

A murmur rippled through the crowd as Monica and Desmond exited the tent; curious guests exchanged questioning glances.

Olivia realized she had to act now, or the opportunity would be lost forever. She hurried toward the officer leading Desmond away. "Wait, officer! Can I have one minute with him? I have some… information… you both need to hear." The officer gave her a questioning look but relented, gesturing for her to go ahead.

Olivia fumbled in her bag for Noah's phone, heart pounding as she swiped through the screen, praying she could get it to play. She found the voicemail and clicked the play button, holding the phone up to Desmond and the officer. Silence hung in the air for a second, and then Monica's voice cut through, dripping with venom and condescension. Monica's head snapped up, her eyes burning with hatred. "You little…" she hissed, but

Olivia ignored her, keeping her focus on Desmond as his expression shifted, the shock and disbelief clear on his face.

The shock, the confusion, and the horror that flashed across his features made it clear—he had no idea what Monica had done. He was hearing it for the first time. As the voicemail ended, Desmond stood frozen for a moment, his entire body tense with barely controlled fury.

"I'm sorry you had to find out this way," Olivia said, watching him struggle to process the betrayal.

Desmond gave her a weak nod, his gaze now locked on his sister. The rage was unmistakable, but he couldn't find the words as he let the officer lead him away.

The officer holding Monica looked at Olivia. "I'm going to need that phone," he said. "I will come back for it after I get Ms. Montgomery in the car." Olivia nodded, kicking herself for getting Noah's phone confiscated.

Now, with Desmond walking away, Olivia's next move was clear. She had to find Jill.

Olivia made her way to Jill, who remained frozen in place, shock coursing through her as she processed the whirlwind of events. "Jill, we need to talk," Olivia said, taking her hand and leading the disheartened bride out of the tent.

In an effort to ease the awkward tension that had settled over the room, the DJ started playing a party favorite and making jokes; hoping to bring back the upbeat atmosphere that had been destroyed.

Once outside the tent, Jill stared into the distance as if hoping the beauty of the gardens and the expansive forest could ground her.

"What just happened?" she asked, turning to Olivia with wide eyes. "Do you know what happened?"

Olivia hesitated, unsure of how much she should divulge at that moment.

"I knew something wasn't right," she started, taking a breath. "When Chardonnay went missing, I was obviously worried, since she had been in my care. I started looking around, trying to figure out where she might have gone. Finding her would have been easy if she had just wandered off or if it was something straightforward. I don't think she would have gone far; she isn't the type to go looking for an adventure."

"That she was gone without a trace made me think someone had taken her. But I had no idea who it was. I started looking at the other guest cottages and overheard several conversations that didn't seem wedding-related. And that the journalist, Thomas, was here didn't quite add up either. I kept noticing bits and pieces that didn't sit right, and eventually, I put everything together. You heard the story from Monica and Desmond, but the piece that didn't quite make it into their retelling was that

Monica took Chardonnay. She hid her in one of the empty cottages. Their plan used her as a distraction, diverting your attention while Monica and Desmond finalized their business deal. When I found her, someone had sedated her and hadn't kept her in her usual living arrangements, but otherwise, she was fine. I got her cleaned up with the groomer and brought her back to you."

The anger bubbling within Jill was palpable. "That little... I never liked her. Neither did Chardonnay. I should have known something wasn't right when Chardonnay didn't like her. Dogs are better judges of character than people are." Jill swirled the bit of champagne left in the glass she was still holding.

"Did you say something about that reporter?" Jill asked, as an ambulance pulled into the circular drive, the medical technicians hastily heading down the hill.

Olivia sighed. "It was Thomas. Monica poisoned him with one of the exotic plants you had on hand."

Jill gasped. "The Meriwether lily?"

Olivia shrugged. "I guess? The purple lily, her mother's favorite flower? Monica knew exactly how toxic it was and used it to get what she wanted. She kept it within a sedative range for Chardonnay, but Thomas wasn't so lucky. He's alive, but he's in bad shape. I don't think her goal was murder—more like trying to keep him out of the picture. But it sounds like he had dug into her, too, and she didn't like the idea of being exposed. People do strange things when they're backed into a corner."

It was Jill's turn to sigh. "Poor guy," she sniffed, her expression sad. "I wish I could say I was really surprised, but Monica has always seemed slimy to me. She always had too much pull in Desmond's life—now I know why."

She paused for a moment, gathering her thoughts. "What I don't know is what to do about this whole... situation," she gestured toward the estate and the tent, indicating the wedding.

Olivia didn't know how to respond. "The best thing you can do tonight is try to get some sleep and start sorting things out in the morning."

"I guess I can stay here another night," Jill said, looking sadly at the estate. "I'll call a car to pick me up in the morning."

As they stood there, two police officers approached. "Mrs. Montgomery?" one asked, his tone careful.

Jill shot him a steely gaze. "Do not call me that. It is still Hastings."

The officer was caught off guard but refocused his question. "Ms. Hastings, could you come answer a few questions?"

Jill allowed him to lead her away, muttering about how she knew nothing. The second officer turned to Olivia. "You mentioned you have some evidence to share?"

Olivia held up Noah's phone. "Yep, right here."

"Okay, great. Would you mind coming with me so we can look at it?"

"Sure," Olivia replied, taking a step forward. Then she realized she hadn't seen Elmer in a while. "Officer, can you excuse me for a second? I need to find my dog."

As she returned to the reception tent, Olivia called for Elmer, her voice cutting through the thick atmosphere, still charged with tension. Just then, her eyes landed on him. The guests had thinned, and most of the vendors were packing up. She spotted Elmer, glued to Raymond Filtch's side as he broke down the catering table, making sure no scraps hit the ground. Olivia shook her head and smiled, filled with warmth at the sight of her loyal companion.

As she turned back toward the entrance of the tent, she spotted Noah standing just outside.

"Hey!" she called, surprised to see him there. "You heading out?"

"Uh, no," he replied, shrugging. "Jill told me I could stay another night if I needed to, so I didn't have to drive that 'classic' back in the dark."

"Oh, okay," Olivia replied, conscious of the police officer waiting just outside. "Thank you so much for all your help, Noah. I realize I pulled you into a difficult situation without much warning, but I truly appreciate your support."

"No worries," Noah said with a reassuring grin.

After a brief pause, she looked up at him, a hint of hesitation in her voice. "One more favor?"

He chuckled. "I assume it can't be any worse than the last one, so shoot."

She glanced back at Elmer, who was happily sniffing around the buffet table. "Would you mind rounding him up when he's done helping Mr. Filtch and taking him back to the pet cottage?" Olivia fished around in the small bag she had been carrying and handed him the cottage key. "Just leave the key inside. I don't think I'll be too long."

"Got it," Noah said, taking the key.

"Oh, and one more thing," she said sheepishly. "Your phone might be evidence now. Sorry. I promise I'll get it back to you as soon as I can." Noah shook his head with a smile. "Keep it as long as you need." He pulled her phone from his pocket and handed it to her. "You might need yours too." Olivia took it, thanking him once more.

With that, Olivia followed the officer, her heart pounding with a mix of anxiety and adrenaline as the events of the evening sank in.

CHAPTER 25

Olivia stirred awake to the cheerful chirping of birds and sunlight streaming through her window, warming her face. "Ugh," she groaned, rolling onto her side, only to come face-to-snout with a very sleepy Elmer, his big brown eyes blinking sleepily at her. A dull throb in her head served as a persistent reminder of the emotional rollercoaster she had experienced. It felt like a hangover, though she hadn't touched a drop of alcohol all weekend. Was 'emotional hangover' even a thing?

Flashes from the night before replayed in a disjointed montage: explosive confessions at the reception, Jill's devastated expression, and her lengthy discussions with the police officer about the chaos that had unfolded. She recalled the rush of the ambulance as they arrived to check on Thomas, who had become gravely ill from the poisoned tea. The medical team had intervened just in time, ensuring he received the care he needed.

Sitting up, she rubbed her face, realizing she was still wearing the dress she'd worn the night before. Somehow, exhaustion had won over any impulse to change into pajamas. A sharp knock at the door jostled her from her thoughts, pulling her back to the present.

Shuffling over, she opened the door to find Shara standing there, bright-eyed and fresh-faced. "Oh right," Olivia recalled with a hint of amusement, remembering that people were going to be here to collect their pets. *My duties to the pampered pets are done,* she thought to herself.

"Good morning!" Shara chirped, her voice dripping with forced cheerfulness. "I'm here to pick up Ayla and hit the road. I'm sure she's ready to go home. I know I am!"

She paused for a moment; her smile faltering. "After everything that's happened here, we could all use a change of scenery."

Her eagerness to leave wasn't just about returning to the comforts of home; Olivia could feel the underlying tension, the desire to escape the lingering chaos and the weight of the secrets that had been told.

Ayla's ears perked up at the sound of her owner's voice, trotting over to nuzzle Shara's hand. Olivia gathered the dog's belongings: food, bowls, leashes, and the all-important bag that contained Ayla's skincare routine. With practiced hands, she clipped the leash to Ayla's collar and handed everything off to Shara.

"Thanks so much for taking care of her. I know her routine can be ...demanding," Shara said.

Shara reached into her bag and handed Olivia an envelope. "Just a little something for your troubles."

Olivia accepted the envelope with gratitude, watching as Shara tugged at Ayla's leash. "Come on, pretty girl, let's get out of here!" The dog turned, following her owner without a backward glance.

"One down, three to go," Olivia mused, turning to Elmer, who groaned and rolled over.

With the sound of tranquility momentarily restored, Olivia sank back onto the bed, considering whether to take a quick shower before the next guest arrived. As that thought crossed her mind, another vigorous knock echoed through the cottage.

"Great," she muttered. "Here we go." She reopened the door to find Seth, Chester's owner.

"Did he do ok after that fiasco of a wedding rehearsal?" Seth asked, his gaze darting to the cat lounging in the window.

"A perfect angel!" Olivia replied, her reassuring smile bolstering her words. "I think the excitement of the rehearsal wore him out. And I don't think he was sad about missing the wedding itself."

Seth snorted. "Excitement might be an understatement." Olivia retrieved the cat carrier and opened the door. Chester immediately hopped in, eager for his exit.

Finally, Olivia heard him think with a tinge of relief as she latched the carrier shut.

Olivia handed the carrier over to Seth, along with a small bag containing Chester's essentials. He hesitated, glancing around as if measuring the atmosphere. "Thanks for looking after him during... well, everything," he said, gesturing vaguely to encompass the recent chaos.

Olivia nodded, understanding settling into her expression. "No problem at all."

"Do you do pet sitting outside of this area?" he asked, his tone threaded with hesitation as if worried about overstepping.

"Well, I can," Olivia replied, arching an eyebrow, intrigued.

A moment of silence fell between them as Seth shifted uncomfortably. "I have this, um, thing coming up in a couple of months," he began, fingers fidgeting restlessly. "And I was wondering if you could watch Chester. I know he's more comfortable at home, and I hate leaving him at those boarding places."

Her face brightened at the prospect. "I'd love to help! Call or text me when it gets closer," she said, scribbling her number on a sticky note she found in the desk drawer.

"Great!" he exclaimed, shoving the note into his pocket with a relieved smile. "Thank you again." As he turned to leave, a thought struck him, stopping him in his tracks.

"Wait!" he called, returning to the doorway. He pulled a wad of cash from his pocket and thrust it toward her. "Here."

"Uh, thanks!" Olivia took the money, surprised by the gesture.

Seth picked up the carrier, his expression sincere. "See you around, then!" With that, headed up the path to the main house.

Olivia put the money in her purse as another knock echoed through the cottage.

"Who's next?" she wondered aloud, heading to the door. Through the peephole, she saw Katherine, Tulip's owner, smiling broadly on the porch.

"Here to get my baby!" Katherine sang, her voice full of enthusiasm. Tulip squawked in delight upon seeing her owner flapping her wings excitedly.

Katherine breezed into the room, her energy palpable as she swooped in to collect Tulip's cage and belongings. "Thanks so much for watching my girl! I'm glad you at least got to see her talents at the rehearsal dinner."

Olivia levied a gentle smile. "Yes, she is quite the performer," she agreed, amused by the thought of the entertainment Tulip had provided at the rehearsal dinner.

"Well, we really must hurry! Our car to the airport is waiting," Katherine continued, her pace hurried.

"Wait, you fly with her?" Olivia's eyebrows shot up in surprise.

"Of course! We fly private," Katherine said, as if discussing a common grocery run. She pressed a couple of crisp bills into Olivia's hand. "Bye-bye, Sweetheart!"

"Bye, Tulip!" Olivia called, holding the door open for Katherine and the parrot to exit. "Bye-bye!" squawked Tulip.

Olivia didn't even close the door before spotting Rachel sprinting down the path, Benny's owner.

"Just need to get Benny!" Rachel called out, urgency in her voice. "The taxi is already here!"

Benny, hearing his owner's voice, sprang up from his cozy spot and bounded into Rachel's arms, snuggling into the purse-like carrier she had ready. He seemed thrilled to be going home.

"Thanks for everything!" Rachel said, a tentative smile brightening her face as Olivia handed over Benny's leash and other belongings. "He's a handful, I know!" she added, casting a glance at the dozing pup. This was one of the few times she had seen Benny stop moving the entire weekend. The weekend must have worn him out.

"He certainly has energy, but I'm sure he'll enjoy being home," Olivia replied, a secret surge of relief washing over her with the final pet departure.

Rachel handed Olivia an envelope, expressing her gratitude once more before turning to leave.

Olivia closed the door with a sigh of accomplishment. "That's the last of them." She turned to Elmer, who was still sprawled across the bed, oblivious to the world around him.

Just as she contemplated squeezing in a brief shower before heading home, another sharp knock startled her from her thoughts.

"Who could this be?" she wondered aloud, her curiosity piqued as she approached the door. She peeked through the peephole once more—her heart leaped as she spotted Noah standing on the porch.

Opening the door, Olivia suddenly became acutely aware of her disheveled appearance, smoothing down her hair and attempting to straighten her wrinkled dress.

"Hey, Noah," she said, her voice light despite the chaos in her mind.

"Hey," he replied, recognition glimmering in his eyes as he took her in. "Rough night, huh?"

Olivia chuckled, shaking her head. "Something like that."

Noah smirked, amusement dancing in his gaze. "Well, I just wanted to say goodbye before I head out."

"Oh! You, too?", she responded, glancing back inside the cottage, now poignantly removed from the events hours earlier. "Elmer and I are leaving soon as well. What are you planning to do with the Rolls?"

"Well, Jill bought it before the wedding, and last night she mentioned donating it to some charity. I told her to call me when she's ready. Until then, it'll just sit at the garage," he shrugged, looking bemused by the idea.

"Donating an entire car seems... extravagant," Olivia mused. A thought suddenly struck her, and she retreated into the cottage, leaving Noah standing on the porch. She rummaged through the bag she had used the night before and pulled out Noah's phone. Rushing back to the door, she held it out to him. "I wanted to make sure you got this back as soon as possible. The officers made a copy of the voicemail, so you're all set to take it back."

Noah smiled and slipped the phone into his pocket. "Thanks." They stood there for a moment, their eyes meeting in a quiet, shared understanding. Olivia broke the gaze, looking down at the porch.

"Well, uh, thanks again for everything," she said. It felt like the words weren't enough, but they were all she could muster.

Noah smiled, a hint of warmth in his eyes. "No worries. I'd do anything..." He paused mid-sentence, realizing he was about to say something more personal. "I like to be helpful," he finished with a small, awkward laugh.

Noah looked up the path toward the estate before shaking his head. "Anyway, I'm off. I'm sure I'll see you around town."

"Yeah, it's Emerald Ridge—we can't really miss each other," she replied, smiling.

As Noah reached the bottom of the steps, he turned, looking back up at her. "Hey, Liv?"

"Yeah?" she answered, heart fluttering.

"You looked pretty last night. I just wanted you to know."

With that, he waved and walked away, leaving Olivia standing there with butterflies dancing in her stomach. A simple compliment from Noah managed to bring up emotions she hadn't felt in a long time.

Elmer finally stirred out of his stupor, letting out a low groan as he stretched, shaking off the drowsiness.

Feeling suddenly invigorated and yearning for the familiarity of home, Olivia gathered her belongings and Elmer's. "Come on, Elmer, let's get out of here!" she called, and the dog perked up, tail wagging, as he followed her outside.

CHAPTER 26

The drive back to Emerald Ridge felt endless, but the closer Olivia got to home, the more she longed for the comfort of familiar surroundings. She turned onto the gravel driveway, the Jeep's engine sputtering to a stop. Before she could unbuckle her seatbelt, Elmer sprang over the center console and shot out the driver's side door, his tail wagging like a madman as he raced to the front door.

Olivia laughed softly, shaking her head as she grabbed their bags. "I figured you'd be out of steam after all that excitement," she said, chasing after him. Elmer was already at the door, nose pressed to the frame, impatiently waiting for her to unlock it.

"Hey, Mom!" Olivia called as she stepped inside, squeezing in just behind the eager dog.

Her mother was in the kitchen, chopping herbs, the fragrant scent filling the room. She turned, her face lighting up with a smile. "Hi, Livvy!"

Elmer was already at her side, demanding attention. He jumped up, wagging his tail, causing her to laugh. "Welcome home, Elmer!" she said, running her fingers through his fur. "Wedding weekend over?"

Olivia let out a deep sigh, leaning against the counter. "Thank goodness," she said, rolling her eyes.

"Oh? Was it more eventful than expected?" Her mom raised an eyebrow, curious.

"You could say that," Olivia snorted, memories of the chaos rushing back. "You didn't stay for the wedding?"

Her mom shook her head, a chuckle escaping. "No, after the rehearsal dinner, I was... dismissed," she said, trying to suppress the absurdity of it all. "Apparently, my tarot readings weren't quite the fun and lighthearted experience Jill had hoped."

Olivia couldn't help but laugh, leaning against the counter. "Some people can't handle the truth."

"Wait, does that mean you got fired?" Olivia asked, her eyes widening in playful surprise.

Her mom laughed, shaking her head. "I guess so. But she still paid me. So, it's all good, but I'm pretty sure I won't be getting any high-class clients from that group—they don't enjoy looking into the darker side of their lives."

Olivia grinned. "Can you blame them?"

Her mom shrugged. "I guess not."

"I'm going to drop our stuff off and take a quick shower," Olivia said, glancing at herself. "It feels like I've been in this dress forever."

"Looks like you have too!" Her mom teased, giving Olivia a quick once-over.

Olivia trudged upstairs, Elmer following close behind. She dropped her bag and watched as Elmer rushed to check his food bowl. After a quick inspection, he circled and then collapsed on his bed, soaking in the sun.

Olivia smiled, her exhaustion hitting her in waves. If Elmer was this worn out, then it truly had been a wild weekend. She headed to the bathroom, already looking forward to the comfort of warm water and the chance to scrub away the chaos.

Clean and refreshed after a long shower, Olivia returned to her loft. The exhaustion crept back in as she flopped onto her bed, phone in hand. As she scrolled through the news, a headline caught her attention: "High-Power Lawyer with Fake Credentials." Her heart sank as she read about Desmond's fall from grace. The story detailing the scandal surrounding him brought Olivia a pang of sympathy.

"Poor guy," she muttered, shaking her head. She remembered what Jill had told her about the pressure he'd faced from his father. He struggled under the burden of unrealistic expectations. She dropped the phone on the nightstand, crawling under the covers. Despite not having eaten, sleep seemed like the best choice. The pull of the bed enveloped her, and soon, she drifted into a deep slumber, letting the weekend's whirlwind slip away.

Hours later, warm sunlight filtered through the curtains, rousing Olivia from her dreams. The soft ping of her phone broke the silence. She glanced sleepily at the screen. It was a message from Noah.

Noah: *Did you make it back?*

Olivia: *Yeah, a few hours ago. You?*

Noah: *Yeah, dropped the car at the garage and picked up my truck, then came back to the house.*

Olivia: *Glad you made it back safely.*

Noah: *Yeah... I was wondering if you had plans this evening.*

Olivia couldn't help but smile. Noah's way of suggesting plans often had a way of changing her mind.

Olivia: *Not that I know of. I think I may have had enough "plans" over the last few days to last me a month!*

Noah: *LOL, true! Well, if you're interested, I picked up some steaks at the butcher on the way home. I was planning to cook them for Sarah and me tonight, but there's an extra with your name on it if you want it. I'm sure we can find some scraps for Elmer too.*

The thought of steak set off an immediate craving, and Olivia's stomach growled. A quiet evening with good food sounded like exactly what she needed.

Olivia: *Sounds good! What time do you want us to be there?*

Noah: *7 work for you?*

She typed "It's a date" but paused, thinking better of it. Instead, she settled on a simpler response.

Olivia: *We'll be there.*

Noah: *See you then*

With a contented sigh, Olivia tossed her phone aside, sinking back into her bed. "Hey buddy," she called to Elmer, who had been curled up, blissfully unaware of the conversation. "We're going to Noah's for steak tonight!" Elmer's tail thumped happily in response.

After a few more minutes of relaxation, Olivia headed downstairs to tell her mom.

"Hey, Mom!" Olivia called, entering the kitchen, where the comforting smell of cooking filled the air.

"Still here!" her mom responded, stirring something aromatic on the stove.

"New concoction?" Olivia asked, sniffing the air.

"Not exactly," her mom said, her eyes twinkling with mischief. "More of a revamped classic."

Olivia smiled. Her mom was constantly experimenting with herbs. "What's up?" her mom asked, glancing over.

"Oh right! I just wanted to let you know that Elmer and I are going to Noah's for dinner."

Her mom raised an eyebrow, a playful smile curling her lips. "That sounds nice."

"Mom, it's just dinner," Olivia said, rolling her eyes at her mom's teasing.

"I know, I know," her mom replied, still smiling. "I appreciate the heads-up in case I needed to adjust dinner plans, but your brother is working a late shift, so it's just a sandwich or leftovers for me," her mom assured her.

"Okay, Mom, love you," Olivia said, kissing her mom's cheek. "We shouldn't be out too late."

"I won't wait up," her mom replied, winking.

Olivia went back upstairs, the creak of the wooden steps beneath her feet a familiar comfort. Once in her room, she surveyed the mess of weekend attire. Sighing, she gathered the scattered clothing, tossing the rumpled dress into the laundry basket. After a brief search through her closet, she chose a casual, soft blue blouse and well-worn jeans that fit just right. She felt a weight lift as she slipped into the outfit, ready for a more relaxed evening.

"Time for a quick refresh," Olivia said to Elmer, who was sprawled on the floor. She headed to the bathroom, brushing her hair into a loose ponytail, a few strands falling around her face.

After splashing her face with cool water, she caught her reflection in the mirror. "Alright, just a normal dinner," she whispered, though the flutter in her chest suggested otherwise. Thoughts of Noah quickened her pulse, a mix of excitement and nerves building.

With a final touch of mascara and lip gloss, she checked herself one last time. "Not bad," she murmured, smiling. She grabbed her favorite pair of sandals, ready for the night ahead.

Before heading out, Olivia checked the time on her phone. Anticipating a quiet evening with Noah made her feel at ease. She called for Elmer, and he bounded down the stairs to meet her.

"Come on, buddy, it's time to go!"

Elmer trotted alongside her, wagging his tail as they reached the door. Stepping outside, the warm evening air greeted her, a perfect night to roll the windows down.

As Olivia pulled into the driveway of Noah's house, a wave of nostalgia washed over her. During her high school years, she always considered this place a second home. She could still picture the sound of laughter and the warmth of shared meals here, memories etched into her heart. Since Noah's parents had tragically passed, leaving him to care for both the house and his younger sister, Sarah, the place had changed, but the feeling of comfort had never left.

The house stood proudly, an old beauty nestled on a stretch of land just outside Emerald Ridge. Olivia appreciated the quiet charm of the farmstead, and as she stepped out of the Jeep, a pang of recognition struck her.

Noah had poured himself into restoring this place, turning it into something truly special.

Before she could gather her thoughts, Noah's voice rang out from around the corner. "Back here!" His tone carried an excitement that made Olivia smile. Elmer, already expecting food with the smells that lingered in the air, shot out of the vehicle and dashed toward the sound.

As Olivia rounded the corner, she stopped in her tracks. Noah had clearly been busy. Noah had extended the wooden porch, lining the sides with rustic benches, and had hung twinkling fairy lights above, casting a soft glow over the area. The lawn was lush, and Elmer had already claimed a spot in the fading sun, stretching lazily on the grass.

"Wow, Noah! You've really fixed the place up," Olivia remarked, a hint of admiration in her voice.

Noah, standing at the grill, gave a small shrug, pride flickering in his eyes. "Sarah and I like to eat outside whenever we can. I'm better with the grill than I am in the kitchen. It works, though."

Before Olivia could respond, Sarah appeared, her arms loaded with bowls and plates. "Here come the sides!" she said, her hair bouncing with each step.

She set a bowl of chips jend salsa on the table, followed by a creamy potato salad and a fresh green salad. Olivia's mouth watered at the sight of the spread. "Man, I thought I was just coming for a quick dinner, but this is a feast!" Olivia laughed.

Sarah and Noah exchanged a glance. Sarah shrugged. "We like to eat around here," she said matter-of-factly.

Olivia settled into one of the padded benches near the table as the day's tension eased. This was the first time she had relaxed in days, the warmth of the evening surrounding her as the sounds of summer filtered through the air. The simple comfort of this place was a balm for her frayed nerves.

"Here comes the meat!" Noah called, breaking her reverie. He stepped toward the table with a large platter of steaks and grilled corn, the savory aroma wafting through the air.

Sarah had already set the table with plates and utensils, making everything seem inviting.

"Dig in!" Noah grinned.

Elmer, ever the opportunist, jumped up on the bench beside Olivia, his eyes locked on the food. Noah chuckled as he cut up the steak and laid a portion in front of him. Elmer's eyes lit up as he devoured the food, his devotion to Noah clear.

Olivia laughed. "He doesn't even look at me like that!"

The table filled with laughter as they dug into their meal. "This is delicious, Noah! I didn't know you were such an excellent cook," Olivia complimented, genuinely impressed.

"Thanks," Noah replied, though a shadow flickered across his face. "It kind of became a necessity after... after Mom and Dad." His voice faltered for a second, but he shook it off, returning to his plate. "We could only survive on frozen dinners for so long."

Olivia's heart tightened, but she didn't push. The weight of his words hung in the air, and she sensed the sadness that lingered beneath his casual tone.

Not wanting to linger on the heavy subject, Olivia turned her attention to Sarah, who was sharing stories about college life. Noah joined in, talking about running the garage. Olivia listened, trying to feel like she was part of their rhythm again. She hadn't been back long enough to reconnect with many people, but Noah and Sarah were familiar, their conversations easy and comfortable.

Once they finished eating, Sarah got up to fetch dessert, leaving Olivia and Noah alone for a moment. A few minutes later, she returned with bowls of ice cream, and they settled back into their conversation. Elmer shifted on the bench, curling up with his head in Olivia's lap as she absentmindedly petted him, allowing herself to relax further.

Noah turned on a Bluetooth speaker, old tunes from their high school days spilling through the air. The music filled the space between them, and they sang along, laughter rising around them as the evening stretched on.

After a while, Sarah jumped up, a knowing look on her face. "You know what? I think I'll do the dishes and finish up my homework. Goodnight, Olivia! Goodnight, Elmer!" she called, hurrying back inside.

Olivia and Noah exchanged a look, both smiling at Sarah's departure. The last bits of anxiety from the weekend faded as they lingered together, the music playing softly in the background.

Noah held out his hand, his gaze softening as he asked, "Want to dance?" A flutter of excitement stirred in Olivia's chest. She hesitated for just a second before accepting his hand. As he pulled her close, they swayed gently to the music, their movements slow and easy. The soft scent of the evening air mingled with the feeling of Noah's warmth beside her.

In this moment, while resting her head on his shoulder, Olivia sensed the weekend's weight melting away. There was no past, no chaos, just the steady rhythm of their dance. She realized how much had changed since they were teens, and yet, in this moment, it seemed like nothing had changed at all.

Noah glanced down at her with a curious smile. "What's going on in that head of yours?"

"Nothing," Olivia said with a soft laugh, shaking her head. "Just thinking about old times."

He pulled her a little closer, and Olivia's gaze shifted to Elmer, who had rolled over on the bench, his paw over his eyes as if to shield himself from the scene in front of him.

Olivia chuckled and leaned further into Noah's embrace. For the first time in days, she felt like everything was right. No worries, no mysteries to unravel—just the warmth of the moment. She closed her eyes, letting herself be swept up in the simplicity and peace of the moment.

CHAPTER 27

The morning light streamed into Olivia's bedroom, draping everything in a warm glow. As she stirred awake, a rare happiness enveloped her—until she rolled over, and her cheek landed in a damp puddle. The source? Elmer. His giant head laying next to hers on the pillow.

"Ew, Elmer! Gross!" she groaned, springing into a sitting position, wiping her cheek with the back of her hand. The dog blinked at her through sleepy eyes, undeterred by her protests, before rolling onto his other side, ignoring her indignation entirely.

"Ugh," she huffed, chuckling despite herself. Resigned to the sloppy reality of dog ownership, Olivia swung her legs over the edge of the bed and padded toward the bathroom. The remnants of her enchanting evening with Noah swirled in her mind like a pleasant dream—*could this be the beginning of something more?* Thoughts of their laughter over dinner, the electric moments when their eyes met, made her heart flutter. But as she stood in the steaming shower, alone with her thoughts, lingering questions crept into her mind. *What did it mean? Could they try to make this work again?*

She hesitated, fear twisting in her stomach. The weight of her past decisions pressed down on her—leaving Noah so suddenly after graduation, with little closure, had been one of the hardest things she'd ever done. She'd needed to leave, to explore, to find herself—but it hadn't been fair to him. And now, poised for a fresh start, Olivia questioned if she was able to give Noah what he deserved.

Her thoughts turned inward, reflecting on how much she'd changed since those days—how much she'd learned about herself. She wasn't the same girl who'd left without a word, full of uncertainty and a need for space. But was she different enough to protect him from the parts of her that hadn't fully healed? She wondered if she could open herself up to him again, without repeating the same mistakes.

Noah seemed so content now, his life full of promise, his future ahead of him. He was happy, genuinely happy. A part of her wanted that for herself too, wanted to share that happiness with him. Yet, she feared that striving for independence could cause her to unintentionally hurt him again, causing him to question his worth like she did before.

She closed her eyes, feeling the ache of uncertainty. *What if she wasn't ready? What if the person she was now couldn't offer Noah the relationship he needed?*

With a quiet sigh, Olivia realized that there was no simple answer. She could only move forward, taking each step as it came.

After a refreshing shower, steam enveloped her like a comforting embrace as she followed the enticing smell of breakfast wafting through the house. In the kitchen, she spotted her younger brother, Jake, already seated at the table, buttering slices of toast.

"Just in time!" her mom called, emerging from the kitchen to place a steaming bowl of scrambled eggs alongside a plate of crispy bacon on the table. "Breakfast is served!"

Olivia slid into a chair just as her mom scooped some eggs and a piece of bacon into Elmer's bowl, which he awaited eagerly on the floor. As soon as it touched down, he dove in, egg and bacon flying in all directions, tail wagging with each bite.

"Nice to see someone appreciating breakfast," her mom smiled, watching Elmer scarf down his food with eager enthusiasm. Olivia's heart warmed at the sight. In just a short time, Elmer had become an unexpected source of comfort, his presence a gentle anchor in the whirlwind of emotions she had been navigating.

As she watched him, she couldn't help but reflect on how much he meant to her. The bond they had forged seemed as though it had happened overnight, yet every moment they'd shared had been significant. She remembered the uncertainty when she first took him in—how he had seemed like a stray thread she wasn't sure how to tie into the fabric of her life. But now? He was part of her world in ways she never expected.

Though Elmer would always carry echoes of Emily, his lost owner, he had made this place his own. Olivia found unexpected comfort in his quiet strength and resilience. In moments of chaos or uncertainty, his warm, steady presence soothed her. He didn't ask for much, just affection, attention, and the occasional treat—but he gave so much in return.

Every wag of his tail, every nudge of his head against her hand, served as a reminder to Olivia that, amidst life's chaos, there were reliable constants she could depend on. And in a life that often felt like it was teetering on the edge, Elmer had become one of those rare, unshakeable things.

Olivia's smile softened as she reached down to scratch behind his ears. "You're a good boy," she murmured, her heart swelling with gratitude. He was her companion, her confidant, the calm she needed to steady her when the storms of life hit.

The family passed bowls and plates around the table, a well-rehearsed morning ritual that filled the air with the familiar sounds of clinking dishes and laughter. They chewed in comfortable silence, appreciating the homey atmosphere. Finally, her mom broke the stillness.

"Well, that was quite the wedding," she remarked, a knowing twinkle in her eye.

Olivia snorted, rolling her eyes. "You can say that again." She had already filled her family in on the events—the lost dog, the financial scandal, the poisoning, and the potential to crack open a decades-old case of suspicious death.

Jake smiled at her. "You sure have a knack for stumbling into interesting situations, Liv."

"It's not on purpose, I swear! But it keeps things interesting," she replied with a grin.

Their conversation ebbed, absorbed by the comfort of breakfast and family. "So what's next for you, Olivia?" her mom asked, leaning in with curiosity.

Olivia took a moment, pondering her next steps. "Well, one groomsman from the wedding asked if I would pet-sit his cat in a few weeks. Aside from that..." she trailed off.

"Do you think you can do this job without getting yourself into any more trouble?" her mother teased, eyebrow raised with a playful challenge.

Olivia laughed, the sound brightening the room. "I hope so! It would be nice to just pet-sit every once in a while." Their laughter echoed through the kitchen as she continued to enjoy the moment.

After breakfast, Olivia helped her mom clean up the kitchen, their hands moving in tandem as they washed and dried dishes. "Any plans for the morning?" her mom inquired, wiping her hands on a kitchen towel.

"I think I'll head down to Perks and Peaks for a coffee, and who knows what might follow?", Olivia replied with a spark of anticipation.

"Taking Elmer with you?" her mom asked, glancing toward the back porch where Elmer lay sprawled, basking in a sunbeam.

"Nah, I think he needs a break," Olivia decided, smiling at the dog's content expression. Gathering her things, she headed for the door, feeling lighter than she had in days.

She slipped into her Jeep, the familiar rumble of the engine stirring her excitement, the vibrations under her hands and feet grounding her as she pointed the vehicle toward town. The open road stretched ahead, the cool breeze brushing her face through the cracked window, adding to the sense of freedom she hadn't realized she'd been missing.

A few moments later, she parked outside Perks and Peaks, and the rich, inviting aroma of espresso wrapped around her like a warm hug. The scent, thick with chocolate undertones and a hint of cinnamon, made her stomach rumble in anticipation. As she stepped out of the Jeep, the sound of the bell above the door chimed as she entered, and the familiar cozy hum of chatter and clinking mugs filled the air. It felt like slipping into a favorite memory, a comforting routine that soothed her soul.

Ashley stood behind the counter as usual, her hair pulled into a messy bun and a genial smile greeting Olivia as she approached. "Morning, Liv! The usual?" she asked, already reaching for a cup.

"Yep," Olivia replied with a smile, watching as Ashley moved around the coffee machines, pulling shots of espresso and frothing milk. Finding her usual corner booth, Olivia settled in and looked out onto the street, soaking in the vibrant energy of Emerald Ridge. Residents and tourists mingled harmoniously, their laughter mixing with the gentle town ambiance.

Moments later, Olivia looked up as Ashley slid into the booth beside her, drink in hand. "That was quite the wedding weekend, huh?" Ashley remarked, her voice brimming with enthusiasm. She hadn't witnessed the weekend's finale herself, but the stories had swept through the small town like wildfire.

Olivia smiled, a warmth blooming in her chest at the sight of Ashley. Despite everything that had happened in the short time she had been back—the whirlwind wedding weekend, the emotional toll of Emily's loss—it was comforting to reconnect with a familiar face. Ashley's laughter and easygoing nature were a lifeline. It was strange, though, how many things had changed. Emily's absence still felt heavy in the air between them, a constant ache in the back of Olivia's mind. But as Ashley sat there, so lively and present, it reminded her that even after loss, there was room to heal, to laugh, and to rebuild what had been broken. A new chapter, however bittersweet, was taking shape.

"For sure," Olivia replied with a chuckle.

"I don't think I've ever made that many drinks for that many picky people in my life! The tourists aren't even that bad. If anyone mentions 'custom coffee bar' to me again, remind me to run!" Ashley said, shaking her head dramatically before they both burst into laughter.

Olivia's gaze drifted across the shop, settling on a small table tucked into the far corner. It was empty now, but a couple of months ago, Jill and Desmond had sat there, looking every bit the high-class couple that seemed foreign in their little town.

"Remember that classy couple we saw in here a couple of months ago?" Olivia asked, the memory causing her to smile.

"Oh, absolutely! We had so many questions!" Ashley paused for a moment before continuing. "I guess we got our answers."

"Yeah, we had no idea what kind of drama they were going to bring into Emerald Ridge, did we?" Olivia mused, recalling the what had followed in their wake.

Ashley sighed, leaning back in her seat. "No idea at all. So what's next for you?"

A familiar question, Olivia noted with a tiny smile. "I'm pet-sitting again soon; beyond that, no plans. Just taking it day by day."

"Seen Noah lately?" Ashley asked, not so subtly.

"You mean since the wedding?" Olivia's heart raced a little at the mention of his name. She felt her cheeks warm slightly as she answered, "Yeah, Elmer and I went over there for dinner last night."

Ashley's eyebrows shot up, her playful grin widening. "Oh? What's this about?"

"It was nothing!" Olivia blurted out, waving her hands as if to dispel the thought. "Sarah was there too. We just ate and hung out. It was... nice."

The word seemed so insufficient for the warmth stirring inside her, but it was the best she could muster in that moment. "Something about the way you said that makes it sound like it was more than 'nice,'" Ashley prodded, a mischievous sparkle in her eyes.

Olivia fumbled for words, unwilling to start a conversation about the complex feelings she had been wrestling with since reconnecting with Noah. Instead, she focused on the safety of the surface. "Yeah, it was nice to be around friends. The weather was beautiful last night, and Noah is actually a pretty good grill master. Elmer loves him! I'm pretty sure Elmer would choose him over me in a heartbeat if it meant getting a homemade meal every night."

Ashley smiled softly. "You know, he really hasn't dated anyone else since... since you left," she said gently. "I saw him with other girls a few times, but he seemed to just hunker down, devoting himself to Sarah and work." The way Ashley spoke made it clear that she thought there was more to his lack of relationships than just a busy schedule. Olivia mulled over the words, turning them over in her mind as she tried to make sense of what it might mean, or if it meant anything at all.

Just then, the bell above the door chimed, signaling the arrival of another customer. Olivia and Ashley turned to see Noah walk in, their eyes locking for a moment that sent Olivia's heart skipping. She felt a flush creep up her neck, unable to shake the soft thrill that coursed through her.

"Hey, Noah!" Ashley called, hopping up and heading to the counter. "What can I get you this morning?"

Olivia turned her gaze to the window, her heart hammering in her chest as he placed his order. She felt his presence, even from across the room, and it stirred a knot of anticipation in her stomach. Then, out of the corner of her eye, she noticed Noah glancing her way again. His soft smile sent a ripple through her chest.

"Leaving already?" she called out, surprised by the slight tremor in her voice. She hated how eager she sounded, but she couldn't help herself.

"Yeah, unfortunately," he replied, pausing for a moment. His expression softened, as if he wished he didn't need to go. "I've got to meet a client at the shop, and I'm already running late."

"Oh, okay," Olivia managed, trying to mask the disappointment in her voice. She didn't want to seem too affected.

"Sorry to disappoint," Noah smiled, his eyes lingering on hers in a way that made her heart skip.

"I'll call you later?" The words hung in the air, and Olivia nodded without thinking.

"Sure, that works," she said, her voice steady despite the whirlwind of emotions swirling inside her.

As he turned to go, Olivia couldn't help but watch him leave, wishing she had said something more.

"Yeah, things are just 'nice,'" Ashley teased, a knowing grin playing on her lips, watching Olivia's every move.

A slight flush rose on Olivia's cheeks as she met Ashley's gaze, uncertain if she should be embarrassed or defensive. The tension between them—the space they hadn't yet bridged—weighed heavily in the air, and she wasn't sure how to navigate it.

Olivia rolled her eyes, tucked back into the booth, and took a sip of her coffee, thankful for its comforting warmth. She settled into her seat, enjoying the comforting bustle around her, allowing her mind to wander toward the unpredictable future that lay ahead.

In that cozy corner of the coffee shop, the familiar thrill of possibilities came over Olivia—in every sip, every laugh, and every moment she cherished in Emerald Ridge. It was a life rich with connections, both furry and human, and she was ready for whatever adventures awaited her next.

EPILOGUE

Olivia stood in the cozy kitchen, cradling a steaming cup of homemade coffee in her hands. The rich aroma enveloped her, grounding her as she gazed out the window at the sprawling property blanketed in morning light. Elmer lay at her feet, his gentle munching on breakfast filling the air with a comforting rhythm. The peaceful silence wrapped around her, a soothing balm after the whirlwind of the wedding weekend. It felt surreal, almost dreamlike—the wedding, the mystery, the dramatic confrontation—now fading like distant echoes.

With the case now solved and Monica behind bars, Olivia allowed herself a moment to breathe, though the sensation wasn't quite that of relief. The weight of everything—the investigation, the tangled lies, and the people she knew—pressed heavily on her chest. Monica's fraudulent schemes were exposed, causing her carefully constructed facade to collapse instantly. Olivia spent days uncovering the layers, watching as each falsehood crumbled, but now that it was done, the silence in the aftermath was almost deafening.

Desmond's once-successful career, the pinnacle of ambition and charm, collapsed. His seemingly indestructible house of cards came crashing down, and the pieces lay scattered around him. Olivia couldn't help but feel a pang of sympathy. The man was a victim of his sister's machinations, a casualty of ambition gone wrong. It wasn't just the scandal—he'd lost himself in it, and Olivia wondered if he'd ever recover who he had been before the world demanded so much of him.

But what haunted Olivia was the revelation about their parents. Monica's confession revealed a truth that could destroy Desmond: his own sister murdered their parents, the people he once admired and perhaps sought approval from. The weight of that knowledge would be like a stone in Desmond's chest, sinking into his very soul. Olivia could only imagine how the knowledge of his sister's betrayal would shatter everything he thought he knew about his family, his upbringing, and his place in the world. *Would he ever be able to look at his family legacy the same way again? Would he mourn his parents for who they were, or would the sickening realization of Monica's actions always overshadow their deaths?*

Despite his career aspirations and achievements, Olivia recognized that his most important asset—his self-worth—was irrevocably damaged.

And then there was Jill. She came into the weekend dreaming of a perfect wedding and left it burdened by reality. The revelations destroyed her world, leaving her struggling to rebuild the life she had imagined. Olivia couldn't help but feel for her—the woman wished for so much, yet the universe threw obstacle after obstacle in her path. Still, there was something about Jill's demeanor that surprised Olivia. She found strength and resilience beneath the hurt and shock. The glossy veneer of a dream wedding faded, but Jill weathered the storm in a way suggesting she might emerge stronger.

Olivia considered these thoughts, reflecting on the strange, winding path that led her here. In the end, it was clear that money—despite all its power—couldn't solve everything. It couldn't buy happiness, it couldn't buy loyalty, and it certainly couldn't buy peace. The truth emerged, and with it, the understanding that what people depended on most often also held them back.

Standing here in Emerald Ridge, a sense of peace washed over Olivia. The storm was over, but she recognized the fleeting nature of tranquility in her life, yet for now, she allowed herself to savor this calm. Olivia watched butterflies flit through the wildflowers outside the window. She realized how much her own perspective had shifted in the short time she had been back home. She didn't have the answers, and she didn't know what the future held, but for the first time in a long time, she felt like she was standing on solid ground. Each mystery and triumph led her to discover her true self and her desired future.

This was the first time in a while that her mind wasn't racing with plans and tactics for whatever might come next, and it was a welcome change. The word "nice" flitted through her thoughts, but she sought something deeper, something richer to describe how she felt. That's when she spotted her mother, Cassandra, making her way toward the house from her shop on the opposite side of the property. A smile cracked Olivia's features—there was something calming and grounding about being back here, amidst the familiar routines and warmth of family.

Just as she took another sip of coffee, her phone vibrated in her pocket, breaking the moment. Frowning, she pulled it out, glancing at the screen. An unknown number flashed back at her. A tingle of curiosity danced across her skin, a reminder of the excitement buried beneath the monotony of day-to-day life.

Maybe it was the soothing rhythm of this daily routine she craved, or perhaps it was the thrill of diving headfirst into another adventure waiting just around the corner. Whatever it was, Olivia's pulse quickened, knowing that boredom was not in her near future.

The road ahead stretched out, peaceful for now, yet Olivia's sharp mind buzzed with potential. New mysteries awaited her, accompanied by the promise of more pets in need of care. With Elmer by her side and the sun warming her skin, a quiet confidence grew within her.

Whatever lay ahead, she would face it head-on—just as she always had. It was in her nature to embrace life's challenges, to dig into the unknown and seek the truth, no matter how tangled the path might become.

As these thoughts swirled in her mind, she realized that perhaps this was where she was meant to be all along. The relentless pace of city life, with its chaotic highs and lows, no longer held the appeal it once had. Here, surrounded by her beloved animals and the small-town charm of Emerald Ridge, Olivia found everything she needed—peace, purpose, and a plethora of furry friends to care for.

For now, it was the perfect life. And as she took another sip of her coffee, the warmth settling in her chest, Olivia sensed she was more ready than ever for whatever awaited her in this vibrant community.

See what's next for Olivia and Elmer in Tails of Trouble Book 3, Secrets Underground.

ACKnOWLeDGements

Writing a book is never a solitary journey, and I am immensely grateful to the many people who have supported me along the way.

First and foremost, my husband, for always encouraging my dreams. He has always known that writing a book was a goal of mine and didn't let me talk myself out of it, though I tried many, many times. He continues to be my biggest cheerleader as I dive further into my journeys with Olivia and Elmer. To my son, whose love and encouragement have always been invaluable and who always things my books are the best, without even reading them. To my larger family and friends. for their unwavering encouragement and love. Your belief in me kept the spark alive that I needed to finish this project.

I owe a special thanks to my editor for polishing my words and bringing clarity to my story, my social media, and marking gurus, Shari and Jill, and my cover artist. Also a separate thank you to Shari and Jill for the use of your sweet girl Ayla as inspiration. Your expertise made all the difference.

To anyone and everyone who got a glimpse of the story as it came together, your feedback, encouragement, and shared experiences have been a cornerstone of this process. I couldn't have done it without your honest critiques and enthusiastic support.

Finally, to the readers, for giving this story a chance. For Indie authors, reader support is everything. You make us believe that we can actually do this writing thing and it's beyond encouraging to know that someone, somewhere wants to read your book. You make all the hard work worthwhile.

ALSO BY JENNA MAESON

Tails of Trouble: The Emerald Ridge Mysteries

Shadows on the Ridge

Secrets Underground

www.ingramcontent.com/pod-product-compliance
Lightning Source LLC
Chambersburg PA
CBHW071406300726
48976CB00006B/2003